KB067497

모르는 영역

〈K-픽션〉 시리즈는 한국문학의 젊은 상상력입니다. 최근 발표된 가장 우수하고 흥미로운 작품을 엄선하여 출간하는 〈K-픽션〉은 한국문학의 생생한 현장을 국내외 독자들과 실시간으로 공유하고자 기획되었습니다. 〈바이링궐 에디션 한국 대표 소설〉 시리즈를 통해 검증된 탁월한 번역진이 참여하여 원작의 재미와 품격을 최대한 살린 〈K-픽션〉 시리즈는 매 계절마다 새로운 작품을 선보입니다.

The K-Fiction Series represents the brightest of young imaginative voices in contemporary Korean fiction. This series consists of a wide range of outstanding contemporary Korean short stories that the editorial board of *ASIA* carefully selects each season. These stories are then translated by professional Korean literature translators, all of whom take special care to faithfully convey the pieceså original tones and grace. We hope that, each and every season, these exceptional young Korean voices will delight and challenge all of you, our treasured readers both here and abroad.

K-Fiction Series

모르는 영역
An Unknown Realm

권어선 | 전미세리 옮김
Written by Kwon Yeo-sun
Translated by Jeon Miseli

ASIA
PUBLISHERS

차례

Contents

모르는 영역
An Unknown Realm

다영은 여주에 있다고 했다.

여주라면 명덕이 공을 친 클럽에서 고속도로로 10분 남짓 걸리는 곳이었다. 그는 새벽에 시작한 라운딩을 마치고 일행과 늦은 점심을 먹고 곧바로 집에 돌아가 쉴 생각이었지만 밥을 먹다 누군가가 가져온 보드카를 몇 잔 마시게 됐고 또 누군가에게 이상한 혐오가 일어 혼자 클럽하우스를 빠져나왔다. 근처 카페 주차장에 차를 세우고 야외 테라스에 앉아 얼음을 채운 콜라를 마시며 술이 깨기를 기다리다 아무 이유 없이 다영에게 전화를 걸었다.

"여주엔 왜?"

Da-yong said that she was in Yoju.

Yoju was about ten-minute freeway drive from the country club where he had just played golf. After the round that had begun at daybreak was over, his party had a late lunch together. At first, he thought he would just go back home afterward and get some rest; but during the lunch he happened to drink a few glasses of vodka that a member had brought, and, to make it worse, he somehow got disgusted with another member. So he left the clubhouse by himself, drove to a nearby cafe, and drank a glass of iced Coke on a terrace, trying to sober up. Then he called Da-yong rather impulsively.

다영은 말이 없었다. 우리가 서로 그런 걸 일일이 묻고 답해야 하는 사이인가 회의하는 침묵 같았는데 설사 그렇다 해도 할 수 없었다. 다영은 짧게 한숨을 쉬더니, 도자비엔날레 때문입니다, 했다. 도자…… 비엔날레……? 그가 담배연기를 빨아들이는 사이, 지금 촬영 중이라서요, 하는 말과 함께 전화가 끊겼다. 그는 뚝 끊긴 전화보다 때문입니다, 하는 정중한 말투가 더 신경이 쓰여 담배를 피우다 말고, 녀석 하고는, 혼잣말을 했다.

담배연기는 하늘로 올라갔고 연푸른 하늘을 배경으로 초승달 모양의 낮달이 크림 빛깔로 떠 있었다. 낮달의 바깥 호는 얇고 선명한 데 비해 안의 호는 세상에서 가장 부드러운 톱니무늬로 하늘빛에 묽게 섞여 들고 있었다. 운동 후의 식사, 낮술의 취기, 봄날의 나른함이 겹쳐 그는 선잠에 빠지면서도 이게 어쩐지 저 은은한 낮달 때문이지 싶었고, 이게 죄다 저 뜯긴 솜 같은 낮달 때문입니다…… 낮달 때문입니다…… 하다 잠이 들었다.

깨어났을 때는 한 시간쯤 지나 있었다. 그는 얼음이 녹은 밍밍한 콜라를 마시고 하늘을 보았는데 낮달의 위치가 생각보다 서쪽으로 많이 기울어 있었다. 낮달을 오래 보고 있자니 최면에 걸린 듯했고 문득 자신의 페

"What are you doing there in Yoju?"

Da-yong kept silent for a while. Her silence seemed to question if they were on friendly enough terms to share such information. Even so, there was nothing he could do about it. Da-yong gave a short sigh and said, "I'm here for the Pottery and Porcelain Biennale, sir." Pottery? Porcelain? Biennale? he took a long drag on his cigarette, during which Da-yong said, "I've got to go, now. I'm in the middle of filming," and hung up. He was more bothered by the polite speech she had used than by her cutting him off. He stopped smoking and muttered to himself: "Oh dear! That child..."

Cigarette smoke rose up towards the light-blue sky, where a daytime moon, a cream-colored crescent, was out. Its outer, convex arc was finely and vividly defined, while its inner, concave arc formed the most lithe serration, blending with the color of the sky. Because of the meal after golfing, the drink, and the lazy spring day, he felt drowsy and thought perhaps the lithe daytime moon was to blame. It's all because of that torn-off, cotton ball of a moon, because of that daytime moon, he kept repeating, before he fell asleep.

About an hour later, he woke up. Drinking the Coke, which tasted flat since all the ice had melted,

인팅에서도 색과 기운을 조금씩 뺄 필요가 있다는 생각이 들었다. 더는 세지지 말자 그런 생각. 조금 연해도 된다고, 묽어도 된다고, 빛나지 않아도, 선연하지 않아도, 쨍하지 않아도, 지워질 듯 아슬해도 괜찮다고, 겨우 간신해도…… 그런 생각 끝에 그는 마치 그 생각의 자연스러운 결론이기라도 한 듯 여주에 가기로 마음먹었다. 가서 도자비엔날레도 보고 다영의 얼굴도 보고 저녁이나 같이 먹고 와도 괜찮겠다고.

차에 시동을 걸고 출발하기 전에 전화를 걸었다. 한참만에 전화를 받은 다영은 대번에 부정적인 반응을 보이며 촬영이 언제 끝날지도 모르고 시간 맞추기도 힘든데 괜히 오지 마시라 했다.

"어차피 도자비엔날레도 볼 겸, 간 김에 젊은 사람들 고생하는데 고기 한번 사주고 싶어서 그러지."

다영이 놀란 듯, 우리 팀 다 사주시려고요, 네 명인데요, 했다.

"당연하지."

아, 네, 하고 다영이 말을 멈춘 동안 그는 딸이 감동에 잠긴 줄 알았다. 그런데요…… 그렇게 하는 게 괜히 멋있어 보일 거 같고 그러셔서 그러신 거죠? 그가 어이가

he looked up at the sky and saw that the moon had dropped further to the west, much more than he expected. Staring at it for a long time, he felt hypnotized, and then was struck with the idea that his paintings needed to lose some color and vigor. They shouldn't become more vigorous. It's okay to tone down a bit, to be lighter. They don't need to be that bright, vivid, or stunning. They could even be on the verge of fading or barely visible. In the end, he decided to go to Yoju—as if it was the most natural conclusion to draw from those thoughts. It seemed a good idea to go and visit the Pottery and Porcelain Biennale and have dinner with Da-yong.

He started the car's engine, but before leaving for Yoju, called Da-yong again. She told him right away that she opposed his visit, saying there was no way she could know when the shooting would be over, so it was too difficult to set a time for dinner.

"I want to go see the Biennale anyway. While I'm there, I would like to treat all of you young people who've been working so hard to a barbecue dinner."

Da-yong sounded surprised: "The whole team? There's four of us, you know."

없어, 넌 왜 그렇게 애가, 하는데 다영은 그의 말을 듣지도 않고 그럼요, 하더니 자기들이 묵는 농가 펜션에서 식당도 하니까 거기서 먹자고, 여섯 시로 예약하겠다고, 주소 입력하라고 자기 말만 다르르 쏟아냈다. 그는 입도 뻥긋 못하고 서둘러 다영이 불러주는 펜션 주소를 내비에 입력했다.

농가 펜션 주차장 한복판에 크고 흰 개가 로드킬당한 것처럼 다리를 쭉 뻗고 옆으로 길게 누워 있었다. 죽은 것 같지는 않고 햇볕에 데워진 시멘트 바닥이 따뜻해 땅과의 접촉면을 최대한 넓히고 누워 자는 것 같았다. 명덕은 개를 피해 차를 세우고 농가를 개축한 펜션을 둘러보았다. 식당이 있는 오른편에 길쭉한 흙 마당이 있고 파라솔이 하나 펼쳐져 있었다. 그는 파라솔 아래 앉아 담배를 피웠다. 그새 구름이 끼어 낮달은 보이지 않았고 허공에 꽃씨만 분분 날렸다. 테이블 위에 놓인 재떨이의 뚜껑이 조금 열려 있어 그는 그 틈으로 꽃씨가 들어갈까봐 마음이 초조했다.
흙 마당 아래로 완만하게 경사진 밭에서 반백의 남자 둘이 일을 하고 있었다. 저리 늙어 보여도 자기 또래거

"Of course."

"Oh, I see," she said and fell silent. He thought his daughter was probably impressed by his suggestion, until she broke her silence, "Well, you do this to think you'll look cool, don't you?"

Struck dumb, he began, "Why on earth are you..." But Da-young cut him short and told him to come to a restaurant that was run by the owner of the farmhouse where her team was staying. She added that she would make a reservation at six, and asked him to type the address into his GPS. Da-yong gave him the address and he put it in silently, with no chance to say more.

At the center of the farmhouse parking lot, a big white dog lay on its side, its legs splayed out, as if it were roadkill. As Myong-dok approached the dog, however, he realized it was just sleeping on the cement, warmed by the sun, perhaps lying in that position to make the warmed surface as large as possible. He parked his car carefully, away from the dog, and looked around the rental cottage that had been remodeled from a farmhouse. To the right of the restaurant was a rectangular dirt yard, where a table stood in the shadow of a beach parasol. He sat under the parasol and began smoking. Only

나 아래일 거라고 그는 생각했다. 두 남자는 주차장에 세워둔 트럭에서 연둣빛 비료포대를 어깨에 지고 날라 밭이랑에 적당한 간격으로 늘어놓더니 한 남자가 포대를 커터 칼로 그어 따면 다른 남자가 포대 끝을 잡고 비료를 털어 밭에 쏟아부었다. 밭이 부채꼴로 생긴 데다 누런 흙 위에 커피 빛깔 비료가 소복소복 쌓이니 이제 비만 오면 흡사 거대한 깔때기에 드립 커피를 내리는 모양이 되겠다고 그는 생각했고 그러자 갑자기 진한 커피 생각이 간절했다. 비료포대를 다 딴 남자가 빈 포대를 착착 접어 하나의 포대 안에 집어넣었고 그렇게 불룩해진 빈 포대는 트럭 짐칸에 던져두고 삽 두 자루를 가져와 두 남자가 한 자루씩 쥐고 소복이 쌓인 비료를 한 삽씩 떠 밭에 고루 뿌렸다. 이제 밭은 초콜릿 알갱이가 점점이 박힌 캐러멜 색깔로 변해갔는데 진한 커피를 마시고 입가심으로 먹으면 딱 좋을 성싶었다.

주차장 쪽에서 흰 개가 그를 향해 사분사분 뛰어왔다. 바닥에 쭉 뻗어 자던 개는 아니고 그보다 훨씬 작은 개였는데 아직 어린 티를 벗지 못해 낮잠에서 깬 듯 어리둥절한 표정이었다. 그를 향해 다가오던 개는 그가 의자에서 일어나자 혼비백산하여 도망쳤다. 누가 보면 해코

then did he realize that the sky had gotten cloudy and the daytime moon was no longer visible. Flower seeds were floating in the air. The lid of the ashtray on the table was ajar, which made him worry that the seeds might fall in it.

A slightly inclined field began where the dirt yard ended. Two gray-haired men were working in it. Although they looked quite old, they were probably either his age or even younger, he thought. On their shoulders they carried light-green sacks of fertilizer, from a truck in the parking lot to the field, and then put them down along the furrows at regular intervals. One of the men then cut open each sack with a cutter and the other one held the corners of the sack and shook it, letting the fertilizer pour down onto the field. The fan-shaped field now had coffee-colored fertilizer piled up on its golden yellow soil. He thought all the field needed was rain falling down on it to make it look like a gigantic funnel with coffee dripping from it. The thought made him want a cup of strong coffee. When they finished emptying the sacks, the man with the cutter folded all the sacks neatly, except for one, and crammed all the rest into it. He then threw the bulging sack into the back of the truck and carried two shovels to the field. Soon they be-

지라도 한 줄 알겠다 싶어 그는, 내가 뭘 어쨌다고, 변명하듯 중얼거리고 재떨이 뚜껑을 열어 담배를 끄고 뚜껑을 꼭 덮었다. 도자비엔날레도 둘러보고 근처에서 진한 커피도 한잔 사먹을 겸 그는 다시 주차장을 향해 갔다.

주중이라 도자 행사장은 썰렁했다. 중앙에 있는 원형 판매장 외에 대부분의 야외 천막은 닫혀 있었다. 둘러보는 사람도 거의 없어 바람이 불면 원형 판매장 가장자리에 매달린 소박한 도자기 풍경들만 찰랑거렸다. 도대체 다영의 팀은 여기 와서 뭘 찍고 간 걸까. 마음이 상한 그는 바로 코앞에 있는 신륵사에 들를 계획도 접고 카페를 찾아 무작정 걷기 시작했고 5분쯤 뒤 멀리 낯익은 커피전문점의 로고가 보이자 곧 진한 커피를 마실 생각에 혀뿌리가 뻐근해졌다.

그는 도로로 향한 창가 자리에 앉아 커피를 마셨다. 정류장이 바로 코앞이라 깨끗이 닦인 유리 너머로 도착하는 버스와 타고 내리는 승객들이 손에 잡힐 듯 가깝게 보여 커피를 마시다 버스가 도착하면 곧장 뛰어나가 타도 될 정도였다. 그의 옆자리에는 머리를 푸릇푸릇하게 물들인 청년이 노트북에 악보를 띄워놓고 작업 중이

gan to spread out the piles of fertilizer evenly, one shovelful at a time, covering the field. Now the field's color was changing to caramel dotted with chocolate chips. It looked like something he would have loved to eat, chasing it down with a cup of strong coffee.

A white dog came in a light-footed run towards him from the parking lot. But it was not the one that was sleeping in a long sprawl there. This one was much smaller, still a puppy, and looked dazed, as if it had just woken up from a nap. When he rose from the chair, the puppy stopped in its tracks and ran away helter-skelter. If someone had seen it, he thought, I could be suspected of hurting it. But I've done nothing! he muttered, as if making an excuse. He opened the ashtray lid, stubbed out the cigarette, and put the lid back on firmly. Planning to take a look around the biennale site and buy himself a cup of coffee, he headed for the parking lot.

Since it was a weekday, there were few visitors at the site. Aside from the booths arranged in a circle at the center, most of the outdoor tents were closed. Only the rustic ceramic wind-bells hung around the circumference of the booths would ring whenever a puff of wind swept across the site,

었는데 손을 내젓기도 하고 고개를 전후좌우로 흔들기도 하고 몸을 부르르 떨기도 했다. 창밖으로는 짧게 깎은 머리에 교복을 입은 덩치 큰 남자 고등학생이 정류장 근처를 어정버정 돌아다니며 한 손을 앞으로 쭉 뻗었다 넣었다 하며 혼자 열심히 떠들고 있었다. 언뜻 보면 정신질환을 앓는 듯 보였지만 귀에 이어폰을 꽂은 걸로 보아 누군가와 통화를 하고 있는 것 같았다. 그래도 그의 눈에 제정신으로 보이지 않기는 마찬가지였고 저런 젊은이들이 점점 늘어간다고 그는 우울하게 생각했다. 귀에 이어폰을 꽂고 몸을 움찔거리거나 한 손에 폰을 움켜쥐고 떠들어대는 사람들, 그들은 심지어 커피를 주문할 때마저 하던 일을 그만두려 하지 않았는데, 조금 전 계산대에서 그의 앞에 선 젊은 아가씨 또한, 그니까 오빠 내가 맨날 그랬잖아, 아 톨 사이즈로요, 내 말이 맞아 안 맞아, 응, 왜 대답을 안 해 오빠, 하고 쉴 새 없이 통화하는 바람에 그가 주문하는 소리가 묻혀 그는 직원에게 두 번이나 큰 소리로 에스프레소! 에스프레소! 외쳐야 했다.

커피를 다 마시고 나오려는데 갑자기 세찬 비가 퍼붓기 시작했다. 차는 신륵사 주차장에 있고 우산은 차 안

breaking the silence. What on earth did Da-yong's team film here? Disappointed, he also gave up on his original plan to visit nearby Sinruk Temple, and set out to find a cafe. With no particular place in mind, he had walked along the street for about five minutes when in the distance he saw the logo of a familiar coffee shop. Immediately, the root of his tongue tightened at the anticipation of drinking some strong coffee.

He sat at a table by the window, drinking his coffee. There was a bus stop right in front of the cafe, so people getting on and off the buses looked so close through the clean window he felt he could almost reach out and touch them. In fact, one could wait for the bus while drinking inside the cafe, seeing the bus arrive, run out, and still catch it in time. A young man with dyed green hair was sitting at the next table, with some music on his laptop. He was waving his hands, nodding and shaking his head and sometimes even his whole body. Outside, a high-school-age boy with a large body, in uniform and with a crew cut, was sauntering around the bus stop and talking excitedly to himself, stretching out his hand and pulling it back repeatedly. At a glance, he seemed to be suffering from some sort of a mental illness; but from the

에 있었다. 오래 내릴 비는 아닌 것 같아 그는 조금 기다
려보기로 했다. 잠시 후 빗줄기가 가늘어졌는지 투명한
우산을 쓴 소녀 둘이 우산을 젖혀보고 뭐라고 종알거리
더니 다시 썼다. 길 건너편에 군복을 입은 청년 둘과 사
복 입은 청년 하나가 둘러서서 얘기를 나누고 있었는데
우산을 쓴 사람은 사복 입은 청년 혼자뿐이었다. 군모
를 뒤로 젖혀 쓴 청년이 웃으며 발을 떨었고 잠시 뒤 군
복 둘은 왼쪽 길로 가고 우산을 쓴 청년은 안쪽 길로 들
어갔다. 그 자리가 텅 비고서야 그는 그들이 서 있던 곳
이 길모퉁이였다는 걸 깨달았고 길모퉁이가 저런 헤어
짐에 알맞은 장소라는 것도 깨달았다.

식당 출입문 왼쪽에 신발장이 있는 걸로 보아 신을
먼저 벗고 문을 열고 들어가야 하는 것 같았지만 명덕
은 신을 벗지 않고 문만 열어 안을 들여다보았다. 담근
술이 든 유리병들이 벽을 빼곡하게 채우고 있는 마루
한편에 다영과 그 일행 셋이 미리 와 앉아 있었다. 남자
둘 여자 하나로 다영과 비슷한 또래로 보였는데, 그의
눈엔 무언가 골똘한 생각에 잠긴 듯 고개를 옆으로 기
울이고 손을 이마에 대고 있는 다영의 모습만이 오려낸

earphones in his ears, he was probably talking to someone. To Myong-dok, nevertheless, the boy looked out of his wits; and he felt depressed by the ever-increasing number of young people like that boy. He had often seen youths with earphones jerking their bodies, or talking loudly while holding a cellphone. They never stopped doing it, even when they ordered coffee, like the young woman who had been in front of him at the counter. She continued talking on the phone while making an order: "So, Oppa, I kept telling you, ah, tall size please, am I right or wrong? Yeah. You're not answering my question, Oppa." Her order got buried in her incessant conversation, so she even had to shout "Espresso!" twice to be understood.

When he was about to leave the cafe, there was a sudden downpour. His car was parked in the lot of Sinruk Temple with his umbrella in it. The rain didn't seem to be lasting long, though, so he decided to wait it out. After a while, seeing two girls outside tilt their transparent vinyl umbrellas while saying something, before putting them back over their heads, he assumed that the rain must have eased up a bit. On the other side of the street stood two young men in army uniforms and another young man in plain clothes, talking together. Only the

듯 선명하게 도드라져 보였다. 쓸려 올라간 앞머리가
오두막 처마처럼 비스듬히 떠 있었다. 다영은 잠시 이
마를 문지르다 어느 순간 스르르 오른뺨을 타고 흘러내
리듯 손을 내렸는데 순간 그는 저 애는 저런 것도 닮아
버렸구나 싶어 가슴이 쿵 내려앉았다. 다영이 그를 알
아보고 자리에서 일어났다.

"아빠 왔어?"

예상 못한 무람없는 인사에 그는 당황하여 어어 소리
만 내뱉다 일행이 덩달아 일어서려는 걸 보고 손을 저
어 만류했다.

"일어날 거 없어요, 일어날 거 없어. 요 앞에서 담배
좀 피우려고."

다영이 뭐라고 하기도 전에 일행 중에서 산뜻한 젊은
여자의 목소리가 들려왔다.

"금방 고기 나온다니까 빨리 오세요, 아버님!"

마당 한쪽에서 펜션의 주인으로 보이는 남자가 흰 개
를 나무라고 있었다. 시무룩하게 야단을 맞고 있는 개
는 아까 명덕을 향해 뛰어오다 공연히 기겁을 하여 도
망친 작은 개였다. 남자가 뭐라 뭐라 추궁하는 소리가

young man in plain clothes had an umbrella. One with an army cap cocked laughed, shaking his leg. After a while, the soldiers walked away, taking the street on the left, while the young man with the umbrella turned into a narrower street. When they were all gone, Myong-dok realized that the spot they had been standing was a corner. It also occurred to him that a corner was a perfect place for such a parting.

Seeing the shoe rack on the left-hand side of the restaurant's entrance, he knew that he should take off his shoes before opening the door. But Myong-dok, with his shoes still on, opened the door ajar to look in first. Da-young and three others were seated on one side of the hall, where shelves crammed with bottles of home-brewed liquor covered an entire wall. Besides Da-yong, there were two men and one woman who appeared to be Da-yong's age. To him, only Da-yong stood out. Da-yong sat there, tilting her head to one side, with one hand on her forehead, as if lost in thought. Her bangs swept back by her hand were slanting down in midair like the eaves of a cottage. Da-yong rubbed her forehead with her hand for a moment, then let her hand slide down her right

들렸지만 뭐라고 하는지 알아들을 수 없었다. 남자가 두리번거리며 마당을 한 바퀴 돌더니 명덕을 향해 다가왔다.

"선생님, 안녕하십니까? 어서 오십시오. 그런데 혹시 여기 어디서 빨간 신발 한 짝 못 보셨습니까?"

그는 못 봤다고 대답했다.

"이놈의 개가 빨간 신발 한 짝을 물고 가서 어디다 놔뒀는지 못 찾겠네요."

"개가 신을 물어갔습니까?"

"네. 빨간 신발을 한 짝만. 큰일 났네 이거."

잠깐 뿌린 세찬 비로 흙 마당은 젖어 있었다. 비료를 뿌린 부채꼴 모양의 밭도 짙은 갈색으로 축축이 젖어 있었는데, 그럴 리는 없지만 그에겐 왠지 그 빛이 김이 오르는 뜨거운 갈색으로 생각되었다. 어디에 숨겼건 신은 엉망이 되었을 터였다.

"신발이 한 짝밖에 없으면 그걸 어쩝니까?"

남자가 끌탕을 했다. 그의 생각에도 한 짝만 남은 신은 아무 쓸모가 없겠다. 남자가 무척 아끼던 신인가 보다 싶었다.

"비싼 건 아니어도 그래도……."

cheek. He was startled to see this same habit that his child had picked up. Da-yong saw him and rose from her chair.

"Hi, Dad, you're here."

The unexpected, unceremonious greeting made him embarrassed, so he just kept uttering, "Er...er..." Seeing the others getting up, too, he waved his hand to stop them.

"No need to get up, no need at all. I'll be right back after a smoke."

Before Da-yong could say anything, the young woman told him, in a sonorous voice,

"The meat will be served any minute now, so don't take too long, sir."

In one corner of the yard, a man who looked like the owner of the rental farmhouse was scolding the small white dog, which looked dispirited. It was the puppy that had come running towards him and then suddenly turned tail. He heard the man's voice, but couldn't make out what he was accusing the dog of. The man walked around the yard, looking in here and there, then came towards Myong-dok.

"Hello, sir? Welcome to the restaurant. By the way, have you seen a red shoe somewhere around

남자가 중얼거리다 말고 그의 눈치를 살폈고 그는 딱히 할 말이 없어 잠자코 고개를 끄덕였다. 비싼 건 아니어도 무척 아끼던 신이면…….

"물어드려야겠지요?"

"네?"

"못 찾으면 물어드리긴 해야겠지만 참 그걸 한 짝만 물어갔다고 한 짝만 물어드릴 수도 없고."

그는 갑자기 흥미를 느끼고 물었다.

"사장님 게 아니고 손님 걸 물어간 겁니까, 개가?"

"그럼요. 손님 신발을 물어갔으니까 지금 큰일 났다는 거지요."

그의 입에서 아이고 소리가 절로 나왔다.

"난감하시겠습니다."

"이거 참 보통 난감한 게 아닙니다. 저놈의 개가 어디다 물어놨는지 말을 안 하니, 아니, 못 하니……."

그는 웃음을 참느라 고개를 숙였다.

"찾아보시다 정 안 되면 손님께 잘 말씀드려보세요."

그가 담배를 끄고 들어가려는데 남자가 눈을 빛내며 따라왔다.

"그러니까요, 선생님이 먼저 말씀 좀 해주시면 안 되

here?"

He said he hadn't.

"This naughty dog's stolen a red shoe, but I haven't been able to find it anywhere."

"The dog has stolen shoes?"

"Yes, but just one red shoe. I'm in big trouble now."

The dirt yard was wet with the shower he had been caught in earlier. The fertilized, fan-shaped field also looked wet, tinged with dark brown. It couldn't be real, but for some reason, he perceived the color to be a steamy, hot brown. No matter where the dog had hidden the shoe, it must have been soiled badly.

"What can you do with only one shoe?"

The man seemed worried sick. He also thought the remaining shoe would be completely useless. That pair of shoes must have been the man's favorite, he supposed.

"They're not expensive, but still..."

The man stopped mumbling and studied Myong-dok's face. Myong-dok didn't know what to say, so he just nodded in silence, thinking, "Though inexpensive, if they were his favorite..."

"I should pay for it, shouldn't I?"

"Pardon me?"

겠습니까?"

"제가요?"

"선생님 일행 분이시니까."

"우리 쪽 신입니까?"

"지금 손님이 누가 있습니까? 선생님 일행뿐인데요.
여기 좀 보십시오."

남자가 출입문 옆에 놓인 신발장을 가리켰다.

"여기 다들 두 짝씩인데 이 빨간 신발만 한 짝밖에 없
지 않습니까?"

"그러네요."

그와 남자가 신발장을 위아래로 내리훑고 치훑었지
만 과연 빨간 운동화는 한 짝뿐이었고 다행히 낡았고
비싸 보이지는 않았다.

"그러니까 선생님이 이게 누구 신발인지 먼저 물어보
셔 가지고 말씀 좀 잘해주시면 고맙겠습니다. 제가 열
심히는 찾아보겠습니다만 만에 하나 못 찾으면……."

그는 알았다고 했다. 일단 남자 운동화이니 다영의 것
은 아니었다. 그는 개가 물어가지 못하도록 신발장 높
은 칸에 신을 벗어 얹어놓고 식당 출입문을 열었다. 다
영의 일행은 누구의 신 한 짝이 없어진 줄도 모르고 열

"If I can't find it, I should pay for it. But then, it doesn't feel right to pay for only one shoe."

He suddenly got interested in the matter and asked:

"So, it's not yours? The dog's taken a customer's shoe?"

"Yes, of course. That's why I'm saying I'm in big trouble."

Myong-dok couldn't help uttering, "Oh, my god! I'm so sorry to hear that. It really must be a difficult problem."

"I'm at my wit's end! That silly dog wouldn't tell me, I mean, couldn't tell me where it's taken it."

To suppress his laugh, he bowed his head. He then said, "You'd best talk to the customer, if it's not found in time?"

Having stubbed out the cigarette, Myong-dok was about to enter the restaurant, when the man followed him, his eyes gleaming.

"I wonder, sir, if you can kindly tell the shoe owner about the situation for me, please?"

"You mean me?"

"Since he's one of your party."

"Oh, the shoe belongs to one of them?"

"Who else, sir? There's only your party in the restaurant. Here, take a look, please."

심히 삶은 돼지고기를 먹고 있었다. 호리호리한 체형에 얼굴이 해사한 남자 스태프가 그를 보고 몸을 들썩거리며, 아버님 고기 나왔습니다, 여기 다영 씨 앞에 앉으십시오, 했고 다른 남자 스태프는 너부죽한 얼굴에 거만하게 다리를 뻗은 채 고기를 잔뜩 문 불룩한 얼굴로 그를 올려다볼 뿐이었는데 영락없는 두꺼비 상이었다. 그는 두꺼비와 호리호리 사이에 끼어 앉았다. 가까이에서 보니 맞은편 벽을 가득 채운 술병의 위용이 자못 대단해 그는 저게 다 무슨 술인지 나중에 주인남자에게 물어보리라 생각했다.

"반갑습니다, 아버님."

다영의 옆에 앉은 여자 스태프가 싹싹하게 인사를 했다. 얼굴은 목소리만큼 어리지 않아 다영보다 두서너 살은 들어 보였다.

"나도 반가워요. 그런데 누구 여기 빨간 운동화 신고 온 사람 있어요?"

"저…… 전데요."

고기 때문에 발음이 뭉개진 두꺼비 청년이 말했다.

"그래요? 그쪽 신 한 짝을 개가 물어갔다는데."

"네?"

The man pointed to the shoe rack beside the entrance door.

"All the others are in pairs, but here's only one red sneaker, you see?"

"You're right."

He and the man checked the rack from the bottom shelf to the top one, then from top to bottom once more. But indeed there was only one red sneaker; fortunately, it didn't look expensive.

"I'd appreciate it very much if you could ask them whose is this and explain the situation to the owner for me. I'll do my best to find it, but in case I fail..."

He promised he would. It was a man's sneaker, so at least it wasn't Da-yong's. Putting his shoes on the top shelf of the rack, so the dog couldn't reach them, he pushed the door open. Da-yong and the other members of the team were enjoying the boiled pork, not knowing one of them had lost a shoe. One of the men, with a slender build turned his fair-complexioned face towards Myong-dok and raised himself halfway, saying, "Sir, the meat's been served, please sit here opposite to Da-yong." But the other male staffer, with a broad face, just sat there looking up at him, his cheeks bulging with the meat and his legs stretched out rudely. His

"그래서 신이 한 짝밖에 없답니다."

두꺼비가 작은 눈을 크게 뜨는가 싶더니 어후후훅 우는 듯한 소리를 내며 웃기 시작했고, 이내 다들 웃어댔는데 특히 여자 스태프는 손으로 식탁을 방정맞게 두드리며, 어머, 개가 물어갔대, 개불쌍해, 개억울해, 하며 깔깔거렸다. 다영이 웃다 말고 그를 나무라듯 지그시 보았지만 그는 무슨 영문인지 알 수 없었고 졸지에 늙은 어릿광대가 된 기분이었다.

삶은 돼지고기가 남았다. 두꺼비가 밤에 맥주 마시면서 안주로 먹게 포장해가면 좋겠다고 하자 다영이 재빨리 일어나 식당 여자에게 비닐봉지를 몇 장 얻어와 고기와 쌈 고추 마늘 새우젓 등을 야무지게 담았다. 여자 스태프는 전화를 받는다고 나간 후였고, 호리호리도 잘 먹었습니다 꾸벅 인사를 하고 나갔다. 두꺼비가 몸을 뒤틀며 힘겹게 자리에서 일어나 벽에 세워둔 ㅏ 자 모양의 지지대를 짚고 절뚝거리며 나갔다. 그러니까 두꺼비는 애초부터 빨간 운동화를 한 짝만 신고 왔고 다른 발엔 발목을 보호하는 장화처럼 생긴 깁스용 신발을 신었는데 깁스용 신발이 크고 높아 신발장에 들어가지 않자

broad face instantly reminded Myong-dok of a toad. He sat down between the toad and the slender one. Seen up close, the appearance of the countless liquor bottles that covered an entire wall was overwhelming, and he decided he would ask the restaurant owner what kinds of liquor they all were.

"Nice to meet you, sir." The woman staffer sitting beside Da-yong said affably. Her face didn't look as young as her voice sounded, perhaps two or three years older than Da-yong.

"Nice to meet you, too. By the way, has any one of you come here in red sneakers?"

"It's...it's me, sir." The toad-like man slurred since his mouth was full of meat.

"It's you? I hear that the dog's stolen one of your shoes."

"Pardon me?"

"So now there's only one shoe left."

Widening his small eyes, the man burst out laughing, "Huh-Hu-Hu-Huk," sounding almost like crying. The others joined him immediately, laughing. The other woman was laughing her head off, flippantly rapping on the table and saying, "He says the dog's taken it away. Oh that poor dog! Falsely accused!"

한쪽 옆에, 그것도 하필 쓰레기통 뒤에 잘 보이지 않게 세워두었던 것이다. 주인 남자는 그것도 모르고 애먼 개만 나무랐던 것이고 그도 덩달아 그런 줄로만 알았다. 두꺼비가 다리에 장애가 있는 줄 그가 어찌 알았겠는가. 누명을 쓴 개도 억울하겠지만 그도 공연히 억울했다.

그가 카드를 내밀자 식당 여자가, 현금 없으세요, 물었고 없다고 하자, 우리는 현금이 좋은데, 하며 마지못해 카드를 받았다. 고기를 챙긴 다영이 여자에게 얼마 나왔느냐고 묻자 구만 오천 원이라고 했다.

"구만 오천 원?" 묻는 다영의 목소리가 높았다. "칠만 오천 원 아니고요?"

"아니 무슨…… 구만 오천 원인데."

"왜요? 만 오천 원씩 다섯 명이면 딱 칠만 오천 원인데요?"

"다섯 명 아니고 여섯 명이라고 했잖아?"

"우리가요? 우리 다섯 명이잖아요?"

"그러니까 오기는 다섯 명" 하다 여자는 명덕을 힐끔 보더니 "다섯 분이 오셨는데, 전화로는 여섯 명이라고 했으니까 그렇게 알고 준비했지."

Da-yong stopped laughing and stared at her father, as if to reproach him, but he had no idea what
was going on and felt as though he had turned into
an old clown.

When the dinner was over, there was some leftover boiled pork. The toad face wanted to take it
to the cottage to eat it with beer later that night.
Da-yong got up quickly, went to the lady of the
restaurant, and came back with a few plastic doggy
bags. She then dexterously put the meat, lettuce,
peppers, garlic, and pickled shrimps into them. The
other woman staffer went out to answer the
phone; the slender man also left the restaurant, after bowing his head to Myong-dok to thank him
for the dinner. The toad face, twisting his body,
scrambled to his feet with difficulty, grabbed for
the "F"-shaped crutch leaned against the wall, and
walked on it limping through the doorway. His foot
was in a cast that looked like a high-top boot—he
had been wearing just one red sneaker. The cast
boot was too high to be put in the shoe rack, so he
had left it in a corner of the entrance, and, to make
it worse, hidden it behind a trash can. The restaurant owner, unaware of that fact, had scolded the
poor, innocent dog, and had him believe the dog

"누가요? 제가요?"

"아가씬지 누군지는 모르겠고 전화 건 사람이 그랬거든 분명히. 여섯 명이라고."

"전화 건 사람 저거든요? 저는 분명히 다섯 명이라고 했는데요. 거기 오천 원은 또 왜 붙이세요?"

여자가 밥값은 별도라고 했다.

"와, 나 진짜!"

다영의 눈빛이 심상찮게 변해가는 게 그는 불안했다.

"좋아요! 밥값은 낼 테니까 다섯 명분 팔만 원만 받으세요."

"그게 무슨 소리야? 고기값이 얼마나 들었는데? 우리 아저씨가 고기만 오만 원어치를 끊어왔다고. 그러니까 이렇게 남아서들, 이렇게 싸가잖아, 응?"

다영이 들고 있던 고기 봉지를 식탁에 탁 내려놓았다.

"그럼 이거 안 싸가면 되잖아요?"

"그건 아니지. 삶아논 거를, 그렇게는 안 되지."

"왜 안 돼요?"

이러다간 한도 끝도 없겠다 싶어 그가 끼어들었다.

"사장님, 그냥 계산해주십시오."

"왜 그냥 계산해요? 우리가 잘못한 것도 없는데 왜 바

was to blame. How could he have known that the man had a disabled leg? Although it was the dog that had been falsely accused, he felt somehow that he had been wronged too.

When he handed the lady in the restaurant his credit card, she asked if he had cash. He said no, and the lady took the card reluctantly, saying, "We prefer cash." Having finished bagging the leftovers, Da-yong came over and asked how much it was. The lady answered 95,000 won.

"95,000 won?" asked Da-yong in a high-pitched voice. "Isn't it 75,000 won, though?"

"No, what on earth...it's 95,000 won."

"How can it be? 15,000 won per person, five of us, so it should be exactly 75,000 won, shouldn't it?"

"You said, six people in your party, not five, didn't you?"

"Six? No, only five of us here, as you can see."

"I know, only five have come," she continued after taking a glance at Myong-dok, "Five ladies and gentlemen have come, but you said six on the phone, so we prepared food for six."

"Who said six? I did?"

"I don't know if it was you. But the one who called definitely said six."

가지를 써요?"

"아니, 바가지라니, 고기가 그게 얼마친데 바가지래?"

다영이 또 뭐라고 달려들기 전에 그는 짐짓 엄한 얼굴로 말했다.

"다영아, 그만하고 나가 있어. 아빠가 알아서 계산하고 나갈 테니까."

다영은 그와 여자를 번갈아보다 몸을 돌려 식당을 나갔다. 그는 서명을 하고 다영이 놓고 간 고기 봉지를 들고 나오면서 혹시 여자가 밥값 오천 원이라도 빼주지 않았나 영수증을 확인했지만 에누리 없이 구만 오천 원이었다.

두꺼비와 여자 스태프는 파라솔 아래 앉아 있고 다영과 호리호리는 개 두 마리와 놀고 있었다. 그가 파라솔 쪽으로 가자 두꺼비가 자리에서 일어났다. 같이 피우자고 하자 두꺼비는 막 다 피웠다며 그에게 라이터를 켜들이댔다. 그가 담배에 불을 붙이자 여자 스태프가 의자를 앉기 좋게 끌어다놓았다.

"아버님, 여기 앉으세요. 다영 씨한테서 말씀 많이 들었어요."

"Look! I'm the one who made that call. I most certainly said five. By the way, what is the extra 5,000 for?"

The lady said the extra 5,000 was for the streamed rice.

"Oh my god! It's outrageous!"

Myong-dok felt anxious, watching Da-yong's eyes take on an unusual look.

"Okay, we'll pay for the steamed rice, but the charge should be 80,000 won for the five of us."

"What're you talking about? Do you even know how much the pork cost us? My husband's bought 50,000 won's worth of it from the butcher. That's why you've this much leftovers, right?"

Da-yong dropped the doggy bags on a table with a thud.

"Then we won't take these. Are you satisfied now?"

"No, that doesn't make sense. It's been already cooked. You can't do that."

"Why not?"

It was going to be an endless squabble, so Myong-dok stepped in.

"Lady, just process the bill as it is, please."

"Why d'you let her do that? We haven't done anything wrong. Why do we have to pay through the nose?"

무슨 얘기를 들었다는 건지 궁금했지만 그는 그래요, 하고 말았다.

"말 놓으세요. 편하게 이름도 부르시고요."

그가 눈을 끔뻑거리며 뭐라고 얼버무리려는데 여자 스태프가 깔깔 웃었다.

"우리 이름 다 까먹으셨죠? 다영 씨 말로는 그렇게 이름을 못 외우신다고. 딱 한 번만 더 가르쳐드릴게요. 여기 개가 신 물어갈 뻔한 친구가 김동수 피디, 저기 늘씬한 친구가 유선태, 저는 홍선영이에요. 아셨죠?"

그는 기억할 자신이 없었지만 알았다고 했다.

"제 이름이 선영이잖아요? 선태하고는 선영 선태 남매가 되고요, 다영 씨하고는 선영 다영 자매가 돼요. 완전 양다리 이름! 제 이름만 외우면 세 명 이름은 공짜로 먹고 들어가는 거거든요."

공짜로 먹고 들어가기는커녕 오히려 혼동만 가중되는 느낌이었지만 그는 기계적으로 선영 선태, 선영 다영, 그리고 뜻 없이 두꺼비 피디, 라고 속으로 되뇌었다.

"담배 좀 그만 피워."

언제 왔는지 다영이 그의 손가락에서 담배를 뽑아 재떨이에 눌러 끄는 바람에 그는 놀라 기절할 뻔했다.

"What? Pay through the nose?" the lady rejoined. "How can you say that? I've already told you how much the meat cost us!"

Before Da-yong made the next move, Myong-dok said, deliberately making a stern face, "Da-yong, that's enough. Go outside and wait for me. I'll take care of this."

After looking at him, then the lady, and back at him, Da-yong turned around and walked out of the restaurant. Myong-dok signed the bill and came out, holding the doggy bags that Da-yong had left. On the way out, he double-checked the receipt to see if the lady had given him any discount at all, even 5,000 won for the steamed rice. But it was exactly 95,000 won.

The toad-like man and the woman were sitting under the beach parasol, and Da-yong and the slender one were playing with the two dogs. When he approached the parasol, the toad got to his feet. Myong-dok offered him a cigarette, but he declined, saying that he had just finished smoking one. The man then snapped on a lighter and held it out for him. When he lit his cigarette, the woman pulled a chair towards him.

"Please be seated, sir. We've heard so much

"어머, 저기 달! 벌써 달이 떴네."

홍이 손을 뻗어 아직은 훤한 저녁 하늘을 가리켰다. 과연 거기에 그가 낮에 본 초승달이 한결 밝고 또렷한 빛을 내뿜으며 떠 있었다. 시선을 내리니 서서히 땅거미가 지는 마당가에서 호리호리한 청년이 허리를 굽혀 개들을 쓰다듬고 있었는데 흰 셔츠를 입은 여윈 등이 초승달을 닮았다고 그는 생각했다.

다들 어딘가로 흩어지고 파라솔 아래엔 그들 부녀만 남았다. 그는 담배를 피우고 싶었지만 눈치가 보여 참았다. 하늘을 보고 있던 다영이 뜬금없이, 용두산 공원 기억나세요, 물었다.

"부산 말이냐?"

"거기서 찍은 사진 있잖아요."

그가 어렴풋이 기억하기로 그들 부부가 부산에 살던 시절, 너덧 살 난 다영을 번갈아 업고 안고 걸리고 하여 용두산 공원에 갔던 아주 더운 날이 있었다. 사진을 찍었는지는 기억나지 않았다.

"거기 하늘에 뭐가 희미하게 찍혔는데 엄마가 유에프오라고 했어요. 그거 낮달 맞죠?"

about you from Da-yong."

He wanted to know what they had heard, but ended up just saying, "Oh, have you?"

"Please talk to us like your own children, sir. And please call us by our first names."

He blinked slowly and was about to give a non-committal answer when the woman broke into a laugh.

"You've forgotten our names, haven't you? Da-yong told us all about your difficulty remembering names. I'll tell you just once more. This poor chap here whose shoe was almost stolen by the dog is Dong-su Kim, the producer. That tall and slender one is Son-tae Yu, and I'm Son-yong Hong. Now you know all our names!"

He was not sure at all if he could remember them, but he said yes anyway.

"My name is Son-yong, right? So, Son-yong and Son-tae, we are like brother and sister, name-wise. And Son-yong and Da-yong, we are like two sisters. My name is, so to speak, filling a double role! So, if you can remember my name, the others are thrown in for free."

As far as he was concerned, nothing was thrown in for free—if anything, he was more confused than before. But he kept repeating in his mind mechan-

"모르지 그건."

그의 대답에 다영은 조금 놀란 듯했다.

"어쨌든 유에프오는 아닐 거잖아요?"

"아니야. 그건 우리가 모르는 영역이다."

다영이 아아 신음을 뱉었다.

"이럴 땐 엄마가 이해가 돼."

"그게 무슨 말이냐?"

"그냥 이해가 된다고. 왜 아빠 같은 사람을 만났는지."

"그러지 말았어야 한다는 거냐?"

그가 소심하게 물었다.

"모르죠 그건. 우리가 모르는 영역이죠 그건. 유에프
오보다 더."

다영이 자리에서 일어나며, 벌써 가실 건 아니죠, 물
었다.

"글쎄다."

그는 이대로 가야 할지 다영과 더 시간을 보내야 할
지 알 수 없었다.

"제가 뭐 잠깐 찍고 올 동안 산책 좀 하실래요?"

"아직도 일이 안 끝났니?"

"일은 끝났는데요, 짬나면 각자 뭐든 찍으러 다니거든

46

ically, "Son-yong and Son-tae, Son-yong and Da-yong, and Toad the Producer.

"Please, Dad! You've smoked enough already!"

Da-yong suddenly appeared, snatched the ciga-rette from his fingers, and stubbed it out inside the ashtray. Caught unawares, he was startled.

"Oh, over there, look at the moon! It's already out." Son-yong stretched out her hand and pointed to the evening sky that hadn't yet lost all its light. Indeed, the moon he had seen during the day was casting a much brighter and more vivid light. When he lowered his gaze, he saw the slender man stoop down and stroke the dogs at the edge of the yard. The young man's white-shirted, thin back felt somehow like the crescent moon.

All the others had scattered except for his daughter sitting under the parasol. He wanted to smoke, but suppressed the craving for her sake. Da-yong, who had been looking up at the sky, asked out of the blue, "Remember Mt. Yongdu Park?"

"You mean the one in Busan?"

"We took a picture there, remember?"

He vaguely remembered that, when he and his wife had lived in Busan, they had visited Mt. Yong-

요. 저도 깜깜해지기 전에 돌아다녀보려고요. 여기서 저수지 있는 데까지 별로 안 먼데 한번 다녀오세요."

"저수지는 봐서 뭐하게?"

"그냥……." 다영은 입을 삐죽 내밀더니, "아빠는 뭘 잘 보시니까 어떤가 보시라고요. 어제 가서 몇 장 찍어 봤는데 이상하게 좋더라고요. 카메라로 찍는 거하고 그림은 다르겠지만 그래도 비슷한 데도 좀 있을 거니까."

그럴까 하고 일어선 그는 손을 들어 딸의 어깨를 살짝 쓰다듬었다. 그런 충동적인 동작에 스스로도 놀란 데다 다영도 흠칫하는 기색이어서 그는 얼른 손을 내렸다.

"내가 이런 걸…… 잘 못해서……."

다영은 그의 말을 못 들었는지 참, 하고 손뼉을 치더니 얼마 냈어요, 물었다.

"몰라도 된다."

"양심이 있으면 밥값이라도 빼줬겠죠?"

"알 거 없어."

"뭐야? 다 받은 거야?"

그는 긍정도 부인도 하지 않았다.

"다 받았구나!"

"여섯 명인 줄 알았다잖니? 사람이 살다보면 실수할

du Park on a very hot day, taking turns carrying the young Da-yong on their backs and in their arms, and at times walking with her. He didn't remember whether they had taken pictures or not.

"In that picture, there was something faint in the sky. Mom said that was a UFO. But it was a daytime moon, wasn't it?"

"I'm not sure."

Da-yong seemed a bit surprised at his answer.

"Anyway, it couldn't have been a UFO, could it?"

"Yes, it could. That's a realm unknown to us."

Da-yong let out a groan. "At a time like this, I understand Mom."

"What do you mean by that?"

"I'm just saying I understand why Mom met a man like you, Dad."

"You mean she shouldn't have?" He asked timidly.

"That, I don't know. It's a realm unknown to us. More so than UFOs."

Da-yong stood up and asked him, "You're not leaving just yet, are you?"

"Well…"

He didn't know whether he should leave or spend more time with Da-yong.

"I'll be right back after taking some pictures. Would you like to take a walk while I'm gone?"

수도 있는 거지."

"이게 실수인지 고의인지 아빠가 어떻게 알아? 한번 이렇게 했는데 먹히면 앞으로 또 이렇게 해도 되는 줄 안다고. 난 사람들 그런 게 싫다고."

"이 사람들 상습적으로 바가지 씌우고 그럴 사람들 아니야. 또 한 번인데 어때? 한 번은 그냥 넘어가."

"한 번이니까 괜찮다……." 다영이 팔짱을 꼈다. "한 번이니까 괜찮다, 그냥 넘어가자…… 아버지는 그렇게 생각하시는 거네요? 그렇게 넘어가면 마음이 좋으세요? 한 번은, 한 번은…… 해도 됩니까?"

명덕은 급속도로 굳어가는 다영의 얼굴이 낯설었다.

"왜 해도 됩니까, 한 번은?"

다영은 느닷없이 깩 소리를 지르더니 흙 마당을 가로질러 뛰어갔다. 어디서 나타났는지 큰 개가 따라 뛰었고 덩달아 작은 개도 따라 뛰었다. 흰 개들을 데리고 순식간에 사라지는 딸의 뒷모습을 보면서 그는 도무지 얼떨떨했다. 계산이 안 맞으면 기분이 안 좋을 수야 있지만 그래도 그렇지 이만한 일에 저 애는 왜 저토록이나 화가 나서 꽝꽝 얼고 절절 끓고 하는가, 저런 건 참 안 닮았구나 싶었다. 전처는 감정의 오르내림이 거의 없는

"Haven't you finished today's work?"

"It's finished all right. But we also work individu-ally whenever we have time to spare. I'd like to take a look around before dark, too. The reservoir is not far from here, so why don't you go and have a look?"

"What do I need to see the reservoir for?"

"Well..." Da-yong pouted out her lips and went on, "You've got an eye for things, so go ahead and see it for yourself. I went there yesterday and took some pictures. I can't explain why, but I like them very much. Of course, I know that photos and paintings are not the same, but there must be a few things in common."

He decided to take her up on the suggestion; getting up from the chair, he unwittingly reached out his hand and lightly stroked his daughter on the shoulder. His impulsive gesture not only surprised himself, but also made Da-yong recoil, so he quickly dropped his hand.

"I'm not really good...at this sort of..."

Perhaps Da-yong didn't hear him; she suddenly clapped her hands once, and asked him, "Oh, how much did you pay?"

"You don't need to know that."

"If she has even an ounce of conscience, she

사람이었다. 아니, 감정은 어땠는지 몰라도 표현은 언제나 온건했다. 화가 치밀거나 용납할 수 없는 일이 생기면 잠자코 손으로 이마를 꾹 짚는 버릇이 있었는데 이마를 짚고 천천히 문지르던 손을 스르르 늘어뜨리기까지 그는 얼마나 가슴을 졸였던가. 그는 늘 실수하고 전처는 번번이 용서하던, 용두산보다 더 오래전의 일이었다. 그러고 보니 그가 기억도 못하는 용두산 사진이 어쩌면 그들 부부와 다영이 마지막으로 함께 찍은 사진이었는지 모르겠다는 생각이 얼핏 들었다.

이대로 차를 몰고 가버릴까 하다 명덕은 마음을 바꾸었다. 지금 가면 다영과 언제 다시 보게 될지 몰랐고 또 젊은 사람들에게 꼴도 우스워질 터였고 무엇보다 그의 손에 삶은 돼지고기 봉지가 들려 있었다. 그는 펜션 남자에게 저수지 가는 길을 물었다. 일단 도로를 따라서 십분 넘게 쭉 가시면요……. 들은 대로 걷다 보니 과연 왼쪽에 좁은 흙길이 나타났고 밟기 좋을 정도로 폭신하게 젖은 흙길을 돌아 들어가니 제법 큰 저수지가 나왔다.
저수지 너머 겹겹이 펼쳐진 산들 위로 해가 지고 있었다. 골짜기의 깊은 곳부터 어둠이 깃들기 시작했다.

would have taken off at least 5,000 won for the steamed rice, right?"

"It's none of your business."

"What? She took the whole amount?"

He said neither yes nor no.

"She did take it all!"

"She said she thought there were six of us. We all make mistakes, you know."

"How do you know if it was a mistake or intentional? If you let her do it once, she'll think that she can get away with it in the future. I just hate it when people do that."

"I don't think these people are in the habit of overcharging customers. It's happened this once, so it's no big deal...let's just forget about it."

"It's happened just once, so it's okay..." Da-yong folded her arms. "Just once, so it's no big deal, just forget about it—that's what you think? Do you really feel okay to smooth it over like that? If it's just once, people are allowed to do things like that—if they do it just once?"

Da-yong's face stiffened, which was unfamiliar to him.

"Why is it okay to do wrong, if it's just once?" Da-yong suddenly screamed, and ran away across the dirt yard. Out of nowhere, the dogs appeared. The

그는 가장자리부터 어두워지는 저수지 물과 그 위에 비친 산 그림자가 짙어지다 물감처럼 풀리는 모양을 오래 지켜보았다. 어디선가 새가 날아와 나뭇가지에 내려앉았다. 날갯짓의 급격한 감속, 날개를 접고 사뿐히 가지에 착지하는 모습, 가지의 흔들림과 정지…… 그런 정물적인 상태가 얼마나 지속되었을까, 새는 돌연 가지를 박차고 날아갔고 그 바람에 연한 잎을 소복하게 매단 나뭇가지는 다시 흔들리다 멈추었다. 멍하니 서서 새가 몰고 온 작은 파문과 고요의 회복을 지켜보던 그는 지금 무언가 자신의 내부에서 엄청난 것이 살짝 벌어졌다 다물렸다는 걸 깨달았다. 그는 새가 날아와 앉는 순간부터 나뭇가지가 느꼈을 흥분과 불길한 예감을 고스란히 맛보았다. 새여, 너의 작은 고리 같은 두 발이 나를 움켜잡는 착지로 이만큼 흔들렸으니 네가 나를 놓고 떠나는 순간 나는 또 그만큼 흔들려야 하리. 그 찰나의 감정이 비현실적일 정도로 생생해 그는 거의 고통스러울 지경이었다. 한참 만에 주위를 돌아보니 그저 저수지였다. 그게 무엇인지 알 수 없지만 그에게 왔던 것은 이미 사라져버렸고 다시 반복되지 않을 것이고 영영 지울 수도 없으리라고 그는 침울하게 생각했다. 단 한 번이라

larger dog ran after her, then the smaller dog followed. Watching his daughter disappear, with the two white dogs at her heels, he felt perplexed. If she gets an incorrect bill, she may feel bad about it. That's understandable. Still, is it a big enough deal to get so angry, freezing and boiling over like that? She doesn't take after *her* when it comes to controlling her feelings, he thought. His ex-wife had no emotional ups and downs. Perhaps she experienced them inside, but her outward expression was always mild. When she was angry or unable to tolerate something, she had a habit of pressing her hand hard against her forehead and rubbing it slowly. He remembered how anxious he would become until she finally let her hand slide down from her forehead. A long time ago, even before their visit to Mt. Yongdu, he had always made mistakes and his wife had always forgiven him. A thought flashed across his mind: perhaps the picture of Mt. Yongdu, which he couldn't even remember, could have been the last picture of the three of them together: him, his wife, and Da-yong.

He considered driving away—just like that. Once he did, though, there was no telling when he would be able to see Da-yong again. Further, he

니…… 단 한 번이었다니…… 다영도 이곳에서 이런 무섭도록 강렬한 한 번을 경험한 것일까. 그래서 그에게 은밀한 보물이 묻힌 곳을 알려주듯 이곳으로의 산책을 권유했던 것일까. 순간 다영의 굳은 얼굴이 떠올랐고, 그게 그러니까…… 한 번은…… 한 번은 해도 됩니까 묻던 다영의 말이 식당 여자가 아니라 자신을 향한 것이었을지 모른다는 생각이 들었다. 왜 해도 됩니까, 한 번은? 그는 숨이 막힐 듯한 통증을 느끼고 자갈 위에 주저앉았다. 과연 그렇다.

텅 빈 들판에 노파 혼자 남아 밭일을 하고 있었다. 노파는 호미를 들고 이랑의 흙을 찍어 작년에 심었던 것의 죽은 뿌리를 파내 흰 플라스틱 통에 넣고 있었다. 이랑의 흙에는 아무 표시가 없었지만 일정한 간격으로 심겼기에 노파가 툭툭 찍으면 영락없이 흙덩이를 매단 뿌리뭉치가 뽑혀 나왔다. 동그랗게 팬 자리에 새로운 씨앗이나 모종을 심을 것이다. 툭툭 찍어 뿌리를 뽑아 통에 넣고 옆으로 한 걸음 옮겨 툭툭 찍어 뿌리를 뽑아 통에 넣는 노파의 동작은 굼뜨면서도 능란해 기이한 리듬감을 주었다. 노파는 플라스틱 통이 죽은 뿌리로 가득

might leave an unfavorable impression on the young people. Worst of all, he was the one in charge of the bags of leftovers. In the end, he asked the owner of the rental cottage for direction to the reservoir.

"First, you walk along the road for about ten minutes and..." As he followed the directions, he indeed came to a narrow, curved dirt road on his left; he then strolled along that wet road, which had just the right degree of softness to it to tread on, and finally arrived at a good-sized reservoir.

On the far side of the reservoir, the sun was setting behind range after range of mountains. Dusk began to fall in the depths of the valleys. For a long time he watched darkness spreading from the water's edge towards the center, and the shadows of the mountains on the surface of the water, deepening at first, then dissolving, like paint. A bird flew overhead, coming from somewhere, and alighted on a tree branch: a rapid deceleration of the flapping, the folding of wings, a light landing, the quivering of the branch, then stillness. The stillness held for an indeterminate span of time; then the bird suddenly took a flight, causing the branch, thickly covered with soft leaves, to tremble, until it became still again. Standing there absently, wit-

차면 밭의 가장자리 둑에 가져가 쏟았다. 일 자체는 간단해 보였지만 선 채 허리를 굽히고 하는 일이라 오래 하다보면 멀쩡한 허리도 노파의 각도로 굽을 수밖에 없을 것 같았다. 노파의 굽은 등은 호리호리한 청년의 등과 달리 굴 껍데기처럼 울퉁불퉁해 보였다. 저 노파는 저녁도 먹지 않고 이때껏 일을 하는가.

그가 담배를 꺼내 물고 주머니를 뒤적거리는데 누군가 아버님, 하고 불러 돌아보니 절뚝절뚝 다가오는 실루엣이 두꺼비 청년이었다. 두꺼비는 그게 자신의 임무이기라도 한 듯 묵묵히 라이터를 켜 불을 들이댔고, 그가 같이 피우자고 하자 이번에도 저기서 막 피웠다며 뒤편을 가리켰다. 두꺼비가 가리킨 곳에는 은박 돗자리가 깔려 있고 그 위에 거무스레한 촬영 장비가 놓여 있었다.

"저기 앉으시겠습니까?"

"난 괜찮아요. 그쪽이야말로 다리도 불편한데 앉아요."

"아닙니다, 아버님. 그리고 말씀 놓으세요. 저는 김동숩니다. 그냥 동수야, 편하게 부르세요."

"글쎄 그게……."

nessing the small stir brought about by the bird and the recovery of stillness, he realized that something stupendous had just opened and then closed again inside him. He was able to experience the whole of the excitement and foreboding the branch must have felt, from the moment the bird flew down and perched on it: Bird, when you grab me with your small, ring-like feet, I am shaken this much; when you release me and leave, I will have to be shaken that much again. The emotions he experienced at the moment were so unreally vivid that it almost felt like pain.

When he came to and looked around, he saw only an ordinary reservoir again. He didn't know what had come over him, but he understood it was already gone, and would never be repeated or erased, and the thought made him feel gloomy. Only once in a lifetime—just this once and no more....When Da-yong came here, he wondered, did she also have this terribly intense, once-in-a-lifetime experience? Is that why she recommended that I take a walk here, as if to tell me where a secret treasure was buried? At the moment, Da-yong's stiffened face came to his mind, which compelled him to think over her question: "You mean, you mean to say, people are allowed to do things like that—if they do it just

"그렇게 부르셔야 외워집니다. 외우셔야 부를 수 있는 게 아니고."

"그런가." 그는 웃었다. "그런데 동수 자네는…… 이런 말 물어봐도 되는지 모르겠는데 다리는 어쩌다가……?"

"얼마 전에 발목이 아파서 병원에 가봤더니 인대가 끊어졌대요."

"원래 아픈 건 아니었고?"

"원래 아픈 건 아니었고요, 언제 끊어졌는지 모르겠는데 끊어졌다네요. 수술하기 전까지는 이러고 다녀야 한답니다."

"수술하면 낫긴 한다나?"

"네, 수술하면 낫는대요. 이번 촬영 끝나고 수술 일정 잡으려고요."

그거 다행이라고 말하면서 그는 좀 서운했다. 동수가 선천적으로 다리에 장애가 있는 것도 아닌데 왜 다영은 개가 신 물어간 얘기에 웃다 말고 나무라듯 눈치를 주었는가 말이다.

"근데 동수 자네, 이건 어떻게 생각하나?"

"뭐가요, 아버님?"

"저 할머니가 저녁을 드셨을 거 같은가, 아닌가?"

once?" Perhaps that question was not directed to the lady at the restaurant, but to him: "Why is it okay to do it once?" He was in so much pain that it felt suffocating. Finally, he sat down on the gravel patch of ground. Why indeed...why is a once-in-a-lifetime wrong all right?

In what seemed to be a deserted field, an old woman was working alone. Using a hoe, she struck at a ridge, digging up dead roots from last year, and tossing them into a plastic container. There was no visible sign of where the roots were buried, but since they had been planted at regular intervals, the old woman was, at every stroke, able to dig up a lump of roots with clods of earth hanging from it. In the rootless holes she would either sow seeds or plant seedlings. She struck the ridge lightly, pulled out a lump of roots, tossed it into the container, took a step sideways along the furrow, lightly struck the ground, pulled out another lump, tossed it into the container, and on. The old woman moved sluggishly, and yet dexterously, creating a curious sense of rhythm. When the plastic container became full of dead roots, she took it to the embankment of the field and emptied it. The work itself seemed simple enough, but anyone who has

"아직 안 드셨을걸요. 보통 저녁 드시고는 다시 나와서 일 안 하시거든요. 다 씻고 저녁 드시니까요."

"그렇겠지? 그럼 이걸 저 할머니께 드리는 거는 어떻게 생각하나? 고기에 야채하고 장하고 다 있는데."

그가 고기 봉지를 들어 보였다.

"아, 그건 좀 그런데요."

"그건 좀 그런가?"

"요즘 시골 사람들, 독극물 그런 거에 예민하거든요."

"독극물?" 그는 예상치 못한 말에 웃음을 터뜨렸다. "하긴 생판 모르는 사람이 주는 고기를 개도 아니고……."

순간 그는 말이 잘못 나간 걸 깨닫고 입을 다물었다. 동수가 웃음을 참느라 큭 소리를 냈는데 이번에도 어째 흑 우는 소리처럼 들렸다.

"그런데 아버님, 이 고기가, 아버님이 사셨으니 아버님 소유이긴 하지만, 제가 양보를 못하겠습니다."

"이거 미안하네, 내가 임의로 처분하려고 해서."

"이제 할머니 가시려나 봐요. 손 씻으시는 거 보니 이제 저녁 드시러 가시는 것 같네요."

"그거 잘됐네."

"이제 저희도 갈까요?"

done it, standing in a crouch like that for a long time, is bound to have a back permanently stooped deeply, as was the woman's. Unlike the slender young man's back, her back looked rough like an oyster shell. Is she working this late without eating dinner? he wondered.

When he was rummaging in his pocket, holding a cigarette between his lips, someone called out, "Sir!" He turned around to find a man who was undoubtedly the toad-like young man, judging by the silhouette limping towards him. The man snapped the lighter's flint and held it out for him in silence, as if it were his usual duty. He offered the young man a cigarette, but this time again he said, "I've already smoked one over there," pointing in the direction he had come from. He looked over there and saw a silver-colored mat spread on the ground and some darkish filming equipment on it.

"Would you like to sit over there, sir?"

"No, thank you. But you should go and sit, with a leg in that condition."

"I'm fine, sir. And please talk informally with me. I'm Dong-su Kim. Please call me Dong-su."

"Well, that's..."

"By calling me Dong-su, you'll remember my name. Not the other way around."

"그러세."

동수가 돗자리로 돌아가 장비를 챙겼다.

"내가 잠깐 그거 들고 있을까?"

"그럼 이 숄더리그 좀 잠깐만 들어주실래요?"

동수가 건네준 카메라가 얹힌 숄더리그는 목마나 강아지 로봇 비슷하게 생겼다. 동수가 돗자리를 접어 가방에 넣고 그에게서 숄더리그를 받아 상의를 입듯 뒤집어 썼다. 그는 동수의 절룩이는 걸음에 맞춰 천천히 펜션으로 향했다.

"동수 자네가 피디라니까 말인데 도자비엔날레에 가선 대관절 뭘 찍고 왔나?"

"와, 아버님! 이름은 못 외우시면서 제가 피디라는 건 한 번 듣고 외우셨네요."

"피디는…… 고유명사하고 다르게 의미가 들어가 있으니까."

그건 그러네요, 하더니 동수는 그들이 영동선을 쭉 따라가는 볼거리 기행 다큐를 찍고 있는데 평창올림픽 기간에 특집으로 방영될 예정이라고, 그들도 오늘 도자비엔날레에 갔다 허탕 쳤다면서 주말에 한 번 더 가볼 예정이라고, 다음 행선지는 원주, 횡성 순이 될 거라고 오

"Is that so?" he laughed. "By the way, Dong-su, you...I'm not sure if I may ask a question like this...but what's happened to your leg?"

"Some time ago my ankle hurt, so I went to a hospital and was told the ligament there had snapped."

"So, you weren't born with the condition?"

"No, I wasn't born with it. I don't know when it snapped, but the doctor told me it had snapped. I have to go around like this until I get an operation."

"After the operation, you'll be okay?"

"Yes, afterwards I won't have any problems walking, according to the doctor. So, I'm going to set the date of operation once this shooting is over."

"Good for you!" he said.

But inside he felt he had been unjustly treated. Dong-su was not even born with the leg condition; so why then had Da-yong stopped laughing at the story of the shoe-stealing dog to glare at him with a reproachful look?

"By the way, Dong-su, what do you think of this?"

"Think of what, sir?"

"The grandmother over there, do you think she's already had dinner?"

"Probably she hasn't. Usually people don't come

근자근 설명을 해주었다. 그는 다영이 하는 일이 궁금해 에둘러 물었다.

"자네는 피디고, 그럼 다른 사람들 업무는 어떻게 되나?"

"다큐라는 게 그래요, 아버님. 누가 피디고 카메라고 작가고 섭외고 명목상 정해는 놓는데 그거에 별로 구애받지를 않아요. 같이 모여서 구성 잡고 넷이 같이 움직일 때도 있고 둘씩 조를 짜서 나갈 때도 있고 각자 흩어져서 찍을 때도 있고, 나중에 돌아와서 같이 편집하고, 주로 공동 작업이니까요."

"그렇군." 그리고 그는 어쩔까 하다 물어보았다. "그런데 자네는 왜 재떨이 뚜껑을 조금 열어놓나?"

"네? 제가요?"

"파라솔에 있는 재떨이 뚜껑을 좀 열어놓는 것 같던데."

"아, 그게 제가 그러기는 한 것 같은데, 왜 그랬는지는 잘 모르겠네요. 냄새 빠지라고 그랬나?"

그는 뭐 야외 재떨이니 그럴 수도 있겠다 싶었다. 실내 재떨이라면 절대 용서할 수 없는 일이지만.

"그런데 아버님, 급한 일 없으시면 오늘 하룻밤 묵고

66

out to work after dinner. It's because they wash up first, then have dinner."

"You're probably right. Then what do you think of giving this leftover food to her? The pork, vegetables, and sauces are all in the bags."

He showed the bags to Dong-su.

"Ah, I don't think that's a good idea."

"Not so proper, right?"

"These days, people living in the country, they're quite sensitive about poison and stuff like that."

"Poison?" At the unexpected remark, he burst into laughter, and said, "Well, it makes sense. After all, it's meat given by a complete stranger. Only a dog would..."

Instantly, he realized he had made a mistake and fell silent. Dong-su made a strange noise in his throat, trying to suppress laughter. This time again, it sounded like sobbing.

"By the way, sir, this meat, well, you've paid for it, so technically it's yours. Still, I don't want you to give it away to others."

"Oh, I'm sorry I've tried to dispose of it as I please."

"It looks like the grandmother's leaving the field. Since she's washing her hands, she is probably going back home to have dinner."

가시지요."

"아니 왜?"

"가서 저희가 한두 시간 편집 작업 좀 해야 하는데요, 그동안 아버님은 다영 씨랑 데이트 하시고, 일 끝나면 밤에 저희랑 술 한잔 같이 하셨으면 해서요. 차 가져오셨잖아요, 아버님?"

"차 가져왔지."

"그러니까 주무시고 가세요. 내일 아침에 해장도 하시고요. 여기 해장국 잘하는 데 있어요. 이번엔 저희가 대접할게요."

"다영이가 그러자고 할지 모르겠네."

"와! 우리 다영 씨, 그렇게 안 봤는데 아버님이 우우해서 키우셨나 봐요. 부녀간에 그렇게 격의 없기가 어려운데 부럽습니다, 아버님."

뭐 꼭 그렇지는 않다고 하려다 그는 입을 다물었다. 아버님, 아버님, 소리를 듣고 있자니 동수가 아들 같기도 하고 사위 같기도 했다. 떡두꺼비 같은 아들, 그런 말이 왜 생겼는지 알 것 같기도 했다. 그에게 아들이 있었다면, 이런 생각은 한 번도 해본 적이 없는데 만약 그랬다면, 아들은 그를 이해했을까. 한 번이니까 괜찮다, 그

"Good for her."

"Shall we go back, too?"

"Okay."

Dong-su returned to the mat and packed up the equipment.

"Do you want me to hold it for you?"

"Could you then hold this shoulder rig for a minute, please?"

The camera-mounted shoulder rig that Dong-su handed him looked like a wooden horse or a robot. Putting the folded mat into his bag, Dong-su took the shoulder rig back and pulled it over his head, like it was a jacket. He walked slowly to Dong-su's limping pace towards the cottage.

"Dong-su, since you're a producer, let me ask you a question: What on earth have you filmed at the biennale site?"

"Wow, sir! You don't remember people's names, but you remember that I'm a producer, after hearing that just once."

"Producer...unlike a proper name, has a meaning."

"That makes sense, sir," Dong-su said and went on to explain in detail the purpose of their filming trip: His team was making a travel documentary, focusing on the interesting and accessible sites

렇게 이해해줬을까.

 다영은 그가 펜션에서 묵고 가는 데 대해 아무 의견
도 내지 않았다. 다만 그가 묵을 방에 들어와 여기저기
둘러보더니 그럼 편히 쉬고 계시라고 했다. 그가 이거
가져가라며 거추장스러운 고기 봉지를 내주자 다영은
잠시 봉지를 들고 서 있다 말없이 가버렸다. 동수가 뭐
라고 얘기를 했을 텐데 굳이 편집 일인지 뭔지 하러 가
는 걸 보면 그와 단둘이 있는 게 싫은 것이다. 설사 그렇
다 해도 할 수 없었다.

 그는 한참 동안 창가에 서서 말벌을 지켜보고 있었다.
크고 사납게 생긴 말벌은 유리창 틀을 맴돌며 어떻게든
방으로 들어올 길을 찾고 있는 듯했다. 밖은 도회의 밤
과 달리 칠흑처럼 캄캄했다. 그는 말벌이 들어올까봐
창문도 못 열고 담배를 피웠다. 좁은 방 안을 서성거리
다 침대 옆에 쭈그리고 앉았다. 몸을 틀어 팔을 침대 매
트리스 위에 얹고 그 위에 고개를 파묻는 순간 그는 이
런 시간을 도저히 견딜 수 없다고 생각했다. 이런 시간
이 무엇인지 특정할 수 없었지만 견딜 수 없다는 느낌
만은 분명했고, 아무 일도 없는데 눈물이 날 것 같은 슬

along the Yongdong Line; the completed film would be broadcast as a feature during the Pyongchang Olympic Games; they too had been to the Pottery and Ceramics Biennale, but in vain, so they were planning to visit it once more over the weekend; the next destination on their itinerary was Hoengsong, Wonju.

The father was curious to know what his daughter did in the team, so he asked in a roundabout way: "You're a producer. What then do the others in the team do?"

"That's the thing about documentaries, sir. We all have a role to play—producer, writer, liaison, and so on. But these are in name only—no one sticks to a fixed role. We compose plans together. Sometimes, the four of us work together; other times, in pairs or individually. Later, we gather and do editing together. In the end, it's all about collaboration."

"I see." After a moment's hesitation, the father asked: "By the way, why do you always keep the ashtray lid open?"

"I do? Really?"

"I've noticed you tend to leave the ashtray lid open. I mean the one on the parasol table."

"Ah, that... Probably I've done that, but I can't explain why. Perhaps to get rid of the smell?"

품과 피로를 느꼈다. 그는 자신이 무엇에 화가 났는지 알 수 없었다. 아니, 다영 때문이었다. 저녁에도 그렇게 그에게 모진 소리만 내뱉고 가버리더니 이젠 아주 음악조차 들을 수 없고 방충망도 허술하고 욕실에 거미줄까지 처진 낯선 방에 그를 내팽개쳐 두고 가면서 어떻게 편히 쉬고 계시라 뻔뻔스레 말할 수 있는가. 그렇게 아비는 뒷전이고 쓸데없이 남만 챙기다 결국 제대로 된 대접도 못 받고 평생 궂은일이나 도맡아 하다 죽고 말겠지. 제 어미처럼. 그는 부아가 치밀어 휴대전화를 찾아 문자를 찍었다.

'자야겠다 깨우지 마라.'

그는 자신이 찍은 문자 내용을 물끄러미 보다 전송을 눌렀다. 곧 매정한 답장이 왔다.

'네 그럼 주무세요.'

그는 휴대전화 소리를 죽이고 불을 끄고 침대에 누웠다. 모든 게 거추장스러웠다. 매트리스를 누르는 자기 몸의 무게도, 감은 채 파르르 떨리는 양 눈꺼풀도, 뇌의 틀을 맴도는 말벌 같은 생각들도. 요즘 그는 종종 힘이 들었고 시도 때도 없이 눈물이 났다. 생은 그를 여기까지 데려와놓고 그가 이제 어떻게든 살아보려니까 힘을

He thought it was not so bad since it was an ash-tray placed outside. If it was inside, Dong-su's behavior would be inexcusable.

"By the way, sir, if you don't have any urgent obligation tonight, why don't you stay the night here?"

"But why?"

"We have some editing to do for couple of hours. In the meantime, you may want to enjoy a visit with Da-yong, and afterwards have a drink with us. You've brought your car, haven't you?"

"Yes, I have."

"So why don't you stay and tomorrow morning have some haejang soup to chase hangovers. There's a nearby restaurant famous for its haejang soup. This time, it's our treat."

"I'm not sure if Da-yong would like the idea."

"Oh! It never occurred to me that Da-yong was that kind of person. But now I suspect that you pampered her a bit. It's hard to find a father and his daughter with no reserve between each other. I envy you, sir!"

The father was going to say, "Not necessarily so," but changed his mind. Hearing Dong-su call him "Sir, sir," he felt as if the young man was his son or son-in-law. The expression "a son like *ttok tukkobi*" (literally "rice-cake toad," meaning a sturdy baby boy) oc-

설설 빼며, 이제 그만, 그만 살 준비를 해, 그러는 것 같았다. 희망이 없어, 그는 흐느끼듯 중얼거렸다. 차라리 단칼에 끊어내고 싶다, 증발하고 싶다, 사라지고 싶다, 지금, 이 순간, 이대로…….

실신하듯 그는 잠깐 잠이 들었고 꿈속에서 어디 자꾸 어두운 길로 가고 있었다. 멀리서 누군가 복잡한 기구를 들고 그를 향해 천천히 다가왔다. 그는 그게 카메라라고 확신했다. 나를 찍는 거냐고 묻자 상대방은 고개를 저어 부인하는 몸짓을 하면서도 여전히 그를 찍는 자세로 뚜벅뚜벅 다가왔다. 그는 혈관이 터지도록 주먹을 꼭 쥐었다. 적당한 거리에 들어오기만 하면 저걸 단주먹에 박살 내고 말리라 다짐했지만 검은 목마는 더 이상 다가오지도 멀어지지도 않았다. 그는 주먹을 쥔 채 덜덜 떨며 서 있었는데, 어느 순간 덜덜 떨리는 주먹만 남고 그는 온데간데없이 사라졌다. 아니, 그 자신이 검은 목마의 렌즈가 되어 있었다. 그는 렌즈가 되어 어두운 허공에서 경련하는 자신의 주먹을 미동 없이 내려다보고 있었다.

짧은 잠에서 깨어난 후 그는 거의 자지 못했고 새벽에 깜빡 잠이 들었다 깨어보니 창문을 통해 환한 햇빛

curred to him, and he felt he could now understand why such an expression had come into being. If he had a son, although he'd never really
thought about it, would his son have understood
him? Would his son have told him, "It's all right
since you did it only once"?

Da-yong did not comment on his staying overnight at the cottage. She just came in his room,
looked around, and told him to rest for a while.
When he told her to take the cumbersome bags of
leftovers with her, she stood there for a moment
with the bags in her hand before she left the room
without saying anything. Dong-su must have told
her what he had on his mind for the father and
daughter, but she insisted on joining the team for
editing or some other task. Obviously, she didn't
want to spend time alone with him, he assumed. If
that's what she wants, then so be it!

He stood for a long time watching the wasp outside the window. The large and fierce-looking in-
sect was buzzing around the window frame, perhaps looking frantically for a way in. It was pitch-
black outside, unlike urban nights. Fearing that the
wasp might fly in if he opened the window, he
smoked without opening it. He paced back and

이 사정없이 쏟아져 들어오고 있었다. 커튼조차 없는 방이었다니. 그는 한참 동안 시린 눈을 뜰 수 없었다. 그래도 밤은 지나갔다.

"안녕히 주무셨어요, 아버님?"

명덕이 식당 마루에서 주인 남자에게 유리병에 담긴 술에 대한 장황한 설명을 듣고 나오는데, 마당에서 호리호리한 청년이 여자 스태프와 얘기를 나누다 꾸벅 인사를 했다. 고개를 돌린 여자 스태프도 그에게 고개를 까딱해 보이더니 청년에게 부러 큰 소리로 말했다.

"선태야, 오늘 아침엔 조증이 캉캉 샘솟지 않니? 어제 고기를 푸지게 먹어서 그런가?"

그러면서 그를 슬쩍 보았는데 순간 그는 봐주고 있다고 생각했다. 저 양다리 아가씨가 이 늙은이를 봐주고 있어. 그렇다고 기분이 나쁜 건 아니었다. 그는 파라솔 의자에 앉아 담배를 피워 물며, 저 청년이 선태라면 양다리 이름은 선……영이로군 생각했고, 어려운 퍼즐을 깨끗이 맞춘 듯한 만족감을 느꼈다.

완연히 따뜻한 봄날 아침이었다. 공기 중에 구린 퇴비 냄새와 다디단 꽃향기가 섞여 있었다. 매화는 다 피어

forth in the small room, then squatted beside the bed, twisted his body, and put his arms on the bed. Burying his face in his arms, he thought he could never stand times like this. He was unable to explain exactly what he meant by "times like this"; nevertheless, there was no doubt about his feeling a limit to his perseverance; further, for no apparent reason, he felt extremely tired and on the verge of crying. He didn't know why he was angry. No, that was not true. He knew that Da-yong was the reason. After dinner, she had spat out such heartless things at him before she took off, hanging him out to dry. To top it all, she had abandoned him in this miserable room with no proper bug screens, not to mention the cobwebs in the bathroom. It was so shameless of her to tell him to have a rest in this strange room where he couldn't even listen to music. She always neglected her father and spent her time, unnecessarily, taking care of others. She would die doing all kinds of nasty jobs for those thankless people for the rest of her life. Just like her mother!

In a fit of anger, he took out his cell phone and typed a text to her: "I'm going to sleep, so don't wake me."

He stared at the text for a while, before pressing

꽃잎을 떨구고, 어제만 해도 봉오리를 매단 채였던 개나리와 목련이 만개했고, 벚나무도 희끄무레하니 꽃망울을 벌기 시작했다. 하룻밤 사이에 그냥…… 와장창이네, 하고 그는 중얼거렸다. 단단하던 꽃망울이 순식간에 터지는 모양이 허공의 유리를 깨트리는 형국이기도 하니 영 틀린 말은 아니지 싶었지만, 개화와 와장창이 어울리지 않는다는 건 그도 인정할 수밖에 없었다. 밤새 한꺼번에 폭발하듯 피어난 봄꽃들을 무어라고 해야 좋을지 잠시 말을 고르다 그만두었다. 유학을 마치고 돌아와 말을 찾지 못해 답답해하던 젊은 시절이 떠올랐다.

"조금 있으면 냉이도 캘 수 있겠는데."

마당가를 둘러보던 선영이 말했다.

"언제요?"

등 뒤에서 들려온 다영의 목소리에 그는 얼른 담배를 껐다. 그가 열기 전에 재떨이 뚜껑은 꼭 덮여 있었는데, 어제 그가 덮어둔 그대로인지 그 후에 동수가 피우고 덮어둔 것인지 알 수 없었다.

"일주일이나 열흘쯤?"

"우리 그때 여기 없잖아요?"

"send." Immediately, a cold reply arrived:

"Okay then, good night."

He turned off the cell-phone sound, switched off the light, and lay down. Everything felt burdensome: his own weight pressing down on the mattress, his closed eyelids that quivered, the thoughts that whirled around inside his brain, like a swarm of wasps. For some time now, he had been feeling overburdened, and often shed tears at any occasion. Life had brought him so far, and now, just when he was making an earnest effort to survive, it seemed to drain him dry and tell him, "That's enough for you. Now get ready to quit living." I've no hope, he muttered to himself, which sounded like sobbing. I'd rather cut it off at one stroke with a knife. I wish to vaporize. I wish to vanish. Here, at this very moment, just like this...

He fell asleep, as if in a dead faint, and in a dream he kept walking along a dark road. He saw someone in the distance, who seemed to walk slowly towards him carrying a piece of complicated equipment. He was certain it was a camera. He asked the person if he was taking pictures of him, but the stranger shook his head no. And yet the man still seemed to take pictures of him, trudging closer to him. He clenched his fists tightly, almost

"냉이가 뭐 여기만 있나? 이동하면서 캐면 되지. 시기만 맞추면 돼. 꽃이 피면 못 먹으니까 꽃 피기 전에 캐는게 중요해."

"캐서 뭐하게요?"

"엄마한테 택배로 부쳐주려고. 우리 엄마 그런 거 되게 좋아하거든. 예전에 쑥도 캐서 보내줬더니 그렇게 좋아하더라고."

그는 다영의 얼굴을 볼 수 없어 답답하면서도 한편으로는 안도감이 들었다. 엄마에게 쑥이며 냉이를 캐서 보내주는 딸의 마음 같은 걸 그는 짐작조차 할 수 없었지만, 다영은 어떨지……. 부러울까. 못 가져서 몸서리치게 부러울까. 그러니까 전처가 죽은 지…… 거의 팔년이 다 되어가는데도 다영은 여전히…….

"여기 참새가 죽었다!"

그가 돌아보니 식당 신발장 옆에 동수가 고개를 숙이고 있고 다영이 쪼그리고 앉아 있었다. 어디어디, 하며 선영과 선태가 달려갔고 그도 자리에서 일어나 그쪽으로 갔다.

"몸체가 온전하고 통통한 걸로 봐서 식당 유리에 머리를 부딪쳐 죽었나보군."

bursting his blood vessels. He got ready to smash the horse-like equipment with one blow once it was close enough. However, the black wooden horse neither came closer nor retreated. So he just stood there, his fists clenched, trembling all over. At some moment, his body suddenly vanished into thin air, save for its trembling fists. In fact, he had been transformed into the lens inside the black wooden horse, and was staring down motionlessly at his fists convulsing in the dark in midair.

After waking up from the brief sleep, he stayed awake until he dropped off again, around day-break. He woke up to find bright sunlight pouring mercilessly through the window. This room doesn't even have curtains! He thought. The sunlight smarted his eyes so much he couldn't open them for quite some time. But at last the night was over!

The slender young man had been talking with a female on his team, but when he spotted Myong-dok, he greeted him with a bow:

"Good morning, sir."

Myong-dok was on his way out of the restaurant, having listened to the owner's verbose explanation about the liquor displayed in the glass bottles in the restaurant. The woman also turned her head

그의 말에 동수가, 그럼 사인은 뇌진탕이네요, 했다.
다들 낄낄 웃는데 다영이 깜짝 놀라 외쳤다.

"이거 여기 놔두면 안 돼요, 선배! 아롱이 다롱이 보면
난리 나."

동수가 얼른 손을 내밀어 죽은 참새 꽁지를 붙잡아
들어올렸다.

"저 주세요, 형."

선태가 손을 내밀었다.

"걔들이 못 찾게 멀리 갖다 묻어야 돼."

"네, 형."

동수가 참새 꽁지를 건네자 선태가 건네받았다. 마치
개울가에서 잡은 작은 물고기 꼬리를 잡아 건네주는 소
년들 같다고 그는 생각했다.

주차장으로 배웅 나온 다영이 그럼 가세요, 했고 그는
알았다 들어가라, 했다. 차문을 여는데 다영이 뭐라고
했다.

"뭐?"

다영은 곧바로 대답하지 않았다.

"왜?"

and nodded to him in greeting, then said, deliberately raising her voice:

"Son-tae, don't you feel your manic energy gush-
ing out? Perhaps it's because we ate so much meat
last night, don't you think?"

She then stole a glance at him, at which point he
knew that she was forgiving his failure to show up
the night before. Ah, the "double-role" young lady
is trying to let my mistake pass, he thought, and felt
better. He seated himself at the parasol table and lit
a cigarette, thinking, "If that young man is Son-tae,
then the double-role lady's name must be Son—
yeah, Son-yong." He felt satisfied, as if he had
completed a difficult crossword puzzle.

It was a perfect, warm, spring-day morning. The
air smelled of both the stink of manure and the
sweet fragrance of flowers. The blossoms of Japa-
nese apricot had already bloomed and had now
begun to fall; the previous day's buds of golden
bell and magnolia had come into bloom overnight,
and the buds of cherry trees had just begun to
open, revealing glimpses of their inner fairness.
Wow, overnight they've all gone crash, crash, crash,
he murmured. "Crash" might not be an entirely in-
appropriate word, either, since all those firm buds
bursting open in an instant were a bit like glass

"뭐든 그렇게 맘대로 하신다고요. 다들 해장국 드시고 가라고 붙잡는데 굳이 그냥 가실 건 뭐예요?"

"술도 안 먹었는데 무슨 해장국이냐?"

"그러니까 술도, 어젯밤에 김 선배한테 술 먹자고 약속해놓고 오지도 않고, 맨날 자기 혼자 이랬다저랬다 하니까."

자기 혼자 이랬다저랬다라니, 어떻게 아비에게 저런 얄잡는 표현을 하는지 그는 어이가 없어 차문을 도로 쾅 닫고 돌아섰다.

"그러는 너는, 다른 사람한텐 그렇게 싹싹하면서 나한테는 왜 그리 박하냐? 개가 신 한 짝 물어갔을 때, 아니 물어간 줄 알았을 때도 그렇고……."

다영이 짧게 웃었지만 그는 웃지 않았다.

"여기 주인 사장도 그 신 한 짝 찾아다닌 거 보면 동수 다리 저는 거 모르던데 처음 온 내가 뭘 안다고?"

"어, 김 선배 이름도 아시네?"

"그럼! 동수! 선영! 선태! 다 안다, 내가. 동수 그 친구 수술만 하면 낫는다는데 나만 아주 뭘 모르는 사람처럼 이상하게 노려보고……."

"그건 김 선배 때문이 아니라 아빠가 잘 알지도 못하

shattering in midair. Nonetheless, he had to admit that "blooming" and "crash" were not exactly a well-matched pair. He then began to think about the correct expression for spring buds exploding into full blossom all at once, only to give it up. He remembered the frustration, as a young man back from studying abroad, he had felt whenever he failed to find certain expressions in his mind.

"Soon we'll be able to gather the pickpurse."

"When?" said Son-yong, who had been observing the yard.

As soon as he heard Da-yong's voice, coming from behind him, he stubbed out his cigarette. Before he opened the ashtray, he noticed that the lid was firmly closed. He wondered whether it had stayed that way after he had closed it the day before, or whether Dong-su had closed it after smoking.

"In about a week or ten days."

"But then we won't be here," said Da-yong.

"This is not the only place with the pickpurse, you know. We can get it in other places as we move along. Timing is more important. Once it blooms, we can't eat it. So we should gather it before blooming," said Son-yong.

"What are you going to do with it?" asked Da-

면서 다롱이한테 누명을 씌우니까."

"다롱이가 작은 개냐?"

"네."

"그게 다롱이…… . 아니, 다롱이 누명을 내가 씌웠냐?"

"알았어요."

"알긴 네가 뭘 아니? 어제 술 약속도 안 지켰다고 뭐라 하는데, 밥값 많이 냈다고 그렇게 화를 내고 가버리고, 내 방에 들렀다가도 그렇게 쌩 가버리고, 가서는 연락도 없고, 그런데 내가 뭘 어떻게 하냐? 날 싫어해서 피하는가 싶어 안 간 건데 넌 왜 자꾸 나만 가지고……."

순간 그는 묘한 기시감을 느끼고 말을 멈췄다. 어제 점심을 먹고 반주를 하다 윤화백이 그에게, 진짜 남교수는 왜 자꾸 나만 가지고 그래요, 하고 징징거렸을 때 자신이 느꼈던 지독한 염증이 절절히 떠올랐다. 기운이 쭉 빠지면서 그는 여주엔 도대체 왜 왔는지, 저녁만 사주고 뜨지 않고 뭘 더 찾아먹겠다고 하룻밤까지 묵고 아직껏 미적거리는지 후회가 되었다.

"그게 아니라요."

"됐다, 가 봐라."

yong.

"I want to send it back to my mom by home delivery service. She is very fond of wild herbs like pickpurse. Once I gathered some mugwort and sent it to her, and she was so happy to get it."

He was anxious to see Da-yong's face, but at the same time he felt relieved not to. He couldn't say he knew exactly what went on inside a daughter's mind when she dug up pickpurse and mugwort to send them to her mother. Nevertheless, he tried to imagine how Da-yong might feel at the moment? Was she envious? Desperately envious since she no longer had a mother? It had been almost eight years since his ex-wife's death, and yet his daughter was still...

"Here's a dead sparrow!"

He turned around and saw Dong-su standing beside the shoe rack with his head bowed and Da-yong squatting beside him. "Let me see, let me see!" Son-yong and Son-tae rushed to the spot. He also got up and walked towards them.

"Its body is plump and intact. That means it flew into the window."

At that observation, Dong-su said, "Then the cause of death is a concussion," making them all giggle, except for Da-yong.

그는 도발하듯 주머니에서 담뱃갑을 꺼냈고 다영이 뭐라고 한마디만 하면 있는 대로 퍼부어줄 생각이었다.

"옛날에 엄마가……."

그는 울컥 감정이 복받쳤다.

"넌, 지금, 여기서…… 네 엄마 얘길, 왜 꺼내는 거냐?"

"엄마가 아빠는 먹다 남긴 건 절대 다시 안 먹는대서요."

"그게 뭐를?"

"안주가 고기밖에 없으니까, 밤에 제가 버스 타고 나가서 과일이랑 치즈 사왔다고요."

"뭘 어쨌다고?"

생각과 달리 말이 퉁명스럽게 나왔다.

"여기서 버스 타고 나가서 뭐 사오려면 얼마나 오래 걸리는지 알아요? 버스에서 내려서 걸어오는데 아빠 잔다고 문자 딱 오고 진짜."

"그러게 아빠 차 있는데 왜 버스로 가? 위험하게?"

그는 버럭 소리를 질렀다. 둘은 잠시 말없이 서 있었다. 그는 만지작거리던 담뱃갑을 주머니에 집어넣었다.

"그래도 나는 가련다."

"가세요. 건강하시고요."

"We shouldn't leave it here," she said in a shaken voice. "The two dogs, Arong'ee and Darong'ee, will go crazy if they find it here."

"You're right."

Dong-su snatched up the bird by its tail.

"Give it to me." Son-tae held out his hand.

"Bury it far away where the dogs can't find it." Dong-su instructed him.

"Okay."

Dong-su held out the bird, with its tail pinched between his fingers, and Son-tae took it. In Myong-dok's eyes, those young men looked like boys, one handing to the other a small fish he had caught in a stream.

Da-yong walked her father to the parking lot to see him off. After they had said good-bye, he was opening the car door, when Da-yong muttered something.

"What did you say?" he asked.

Da-yong didn't answer right away.

"What is it?"

"You always have your own way. Everyone wants you to stay and have *haejang* soup, but you insist on leaving....Why?"

"I didn't even drink last night. So why would I

"다영이 너도, 촬영 일정도 긴데, 에너지를 비축하고 파이팅 해라!"

그는 손을 내밀어 딸에게 악수를 청하려다 그만두었다. 다영이 픽 웃었다.

"왜 웃어?"

"그냥 비축 그런 말도 웃기고…… 아빠 만나서 그거 하나는 좋았어요."

"뭐? 고기?"

다영은 들은 척도 않고 식당 쪽 마당을 가리켰다.

"어제 저기서 아빠가 잘 못한다고 말한 거, 그거 좋았다고."

그는 단박에 알아듣고 기분이 좋아졌다.

"그러는 너는, 너도 스킨십 잘 못하면서 뭐가 좋았다고 그래?"

"네? 스킨십 말고 아빠가 내가 이런 거 잘 못한다 그런 거."

"그러니까 친밀하게, 그런 걸 내가 잘 못한다."

"아, 답답해. 그게 아니라, 아빠가, 무엇무엇을, 잘 못한다, 그렇게 인정하는 말, 태도 말이에요."

"아, 그거……."

want to have *haejang* soup?"

"That's what I mean. You promised Dong-su that you would have a drink with us last night, but you didn't come. You're always changing your mind, as you please."

Changing your mind as you please? How could she say such a belittling thing to her own father? Dumbfounded, he slammed the car door and turned to face her.

"What about you? You're so friendly with everyone else, but why are you so callous towards me? When the dog took the shoe, I mean when I mistakenly thought the dog had done it, you were, as usual, unsympathetic..."

Da-yong laughed a little.

"Even the owner was looking all over for that shoe, which means he didn't know about Dong-su's leg either. How then would I, a newcomer, possibly have known it?"

"Wow, you even remember Dong-su's name?"

"Of course, Dong-su! Son-yong! Son-tae! I remember them all. Dong-su said after an operation, his leg would be just fine. But you treated me like a person who has no manners, you even glared at me!"

"That was not because of Dong-su, but because

순간 그는 눈앞이 자욱해지면서 다영의 모습이 흐릿하게 멀어지는 걸 느꼈다. 고개를 들어 하늘을 보았다. 연유 빛으로 부예진 허공에 동글동글한 그물무늬가 아른거렸다. 비문증 때문이겠지만 그는 요즘 유독 눈이 갑갑하고 흐려져 백내장이나 녹내장이 아닌지 의심하고 있었다.

"근데 아빠 물귀신이에요? 왜 맨날, 그러는 너는, 그래?" 하고 툴툴대던 다영이 걱정스레 묻는 소리가 들려왔다. "아빠, 왜요?"

"음…… 내가 요즘 당최 눈이……."

눈에 탁한 눈물이 고여 그는 눈을 깜빡거렸다.

"눈이 잘 안 보여요? 그럼 저기, 달 뜬 거 보여 안 보여? 되게 예쁜 달인데."

"달? 낮달이 또 떴어?"

아무것도 보이지 않았고 아무것도 잡을 수 없었다.

"안 보인다, 다영아."

그는 조금 무서워졌다.

"안 보여, 아빠? 병원에선 뭐래요?"

"응, 이제 가봐야……."

"아버지! 제정신이세요?" 다영의 목소리가 높아졌다.

you falsely accused Darong'ee when you didn't even know the truth."

"Darong'ee is the small dog?"

"Yes."

"Darong'ee....Let me ask you: Am I the one who started the accusation?"

"I know, you didn't start it."

"You know? What on earth do you know? You complain that I didn't keep my promise last night. Now, let's see...first, you got angry because I paid too much for the dinner; second, you came to my room only to dash out again; third, you stayed away without even a phone call. What could I have done? It looked as if you hated me and tried to avoid me. But you keep pointing a finger only at me..."

At the moment, he felt a strange sense of déjàvu, which made him stop talking. While drinking at lunch on the previous day, Yun the painter had complained to him, "Why are you always picking on me?" Now he was remembering how terribly disgusted he had gotten with Yun's complaint. All of a sudden, he felt the life draining out of his body. He regretted coming to Yoju, not leaving Yoju right after paying for the dinner, and staying overnight. What on earth was it that he wanted to gain by

"왜 제때제때 병원을 왜 안 가세요? 어린애세요? 혼자 못 가세요? 안 보여도 음악은 하고 글은 써도 눈멀면 아예 사진 못 찍고 그림 못 그리는 거 모르십니까? 내 참, 기가 막혀서! 생각이 있는 거야 없는……."

다영이 타탁타탁 뛰어가는 소리가 들렸다.

명덕은 심봉사가 된 기분으로 더듬더듬 차문을 열고 차에 타서 글로브박스를 열어 휴지를 꺼내 눈물을 닦았다. 한참 동안 눈을 감았다 뜨기를 반복했다. 뭉글뭉글 뭉개져 보이던 세상이 차츰 제 모습을 되찾았다. 다영이 돌아올까 싶어 차 문을 열어놓고 담배도 피우지 않고 기다렸지만 다영은 오지 않았다. 간다면 간다고 말을 해야지 저 애는 대체 왜 저렇게 제멋대로 생겨먹었는지.

그는 차문을 닫고 시동을 걸었다. 출발하려다 차창 너머로 초승달을 보았다. 어제보다 살이 더 오른 걸로 보아 바야흐로 차는 중인 것 같았다. 그러고 보니 어제부터 오늘까지 그는 누군가의 인생을 일별하듯 아침, 오후, 저녁의 낮달을 모두 보았다. 왜 아침달 낮달 저녁달이 아니고 모두 낮달인가 생각하다, 해 뜨고 뜬 달은 죄

staying overnight and then lingering on in the morning?

"You've got it all wrong, Dad."

"Enough! Now you can go back to your team!"

As if to provoke her, he took out a pack of cigarettes, preparing to give Da-yong another piece of his mind if she spoke again.

"A long time ago, Mom..."

He suddenly became seized with grudges.

"You, now, here...why on earth do you want to talk about your mom?"

"Mom said you never eat leftovers."

"So what?"

"The only thing we had last night was leftovers. So I went out to town by bus and bought some fruit and cheese for you..."

"...what?"

Unlike what he was feeling inside, his interjection was curt.

"Do you know how much time it takes to go there by bus? I got off the bus and was walking back to this place when you sent a text saying you were going to sleep. Perfect timing, Dad!"

"My car was here. Why did you have to take the bus? It was such a dangerous thing to do," he yelled.

다 낮달인 게지, 생각했다. 해는 늘 낮달만 만나고, 그러니 해 입장에서 밤에 뜨는 달은 영영 모르는 거지, 그런 생각을 하며 그는 농가 펜션의 주차장을 빠져나왔다.

And they stood for a while, neither saying anything. He put the cigarette pack he'd been fingering
back in his pocket.

"I'm leaving now anyway."

"Okay. Take care of yourself."

"You, too, Da-yong, be careful not to drain yourself dry. Try to reserve your strength. You've still
got a long way to go until the shooting is over. So
cheer up!"

He was going to hold out his hand to shake with
Da-yong, but quickly changed his mind. Da-yong
grinned.

"What's so funny?"

"The word 'reserve' sounds funny...and there's
one good thing about meeting you."

"What? The meat?"

Da-yong ignored his words and pointed to the
yard in front of the restaurant.

"Over there, you said you weren't good at this
sort of thing. That was nice."

He understood right away and felt better.

"What about you? You're not good at *skinship*, either. So what was so nice about it?"

"What? No, it's not about physical contact. The
fact that you said you were not good at this sort of
thing. That's what I'm talking about."

"Yeah, I know, I'm not good at being friendly with others."

"Oh my god! Not that either, Dad. Your admitting that you are not good at anything. The words and the attitude of acknowledgement. That's what I like."

"Ah, that..."

At that moment, he felt his eyes blurring and couldn't see Da-yong clearly. He lifted his head to look at the sky, but all he could see was what seemed to be a network of circles flickering in the condensed milk-colored air. Lately, his vision had been getting blurry and unclear more than ever, probably because of the floaters in his eyes, but he was not ruling out cataracts or glaucoma.

"You're like a water demon, always dragging me down, do you know that? You always say: 'What about you? What about you?' Why do you do that?"

Da-yong kept on grumbling, until she noticed something wrong with him. "Dad, what's wrong?"

"Well...these days, my eyes are really..."

He kept blinking because of the turbid tears in his eyes.

"You can't see well? Can you see the daytime moon up there? It's beautiful."

"Moon...a daytime moon is out again?"

He couldn't see anything, or find anything to hang onto.

"I can't see, Da-yong."

He got a little frightened.

"You can't see, Dad? What do they say at the hospital?"

"Well, I'm planning to go see a doctor..."

"Dad, are you out of your mind?" she had raised her voice. "Why can't you go to hospital in time? Are you a child? Can't you go by yourself? You may not need eyesight to write or play music; but you'll never be able to take pictures or paint! Don't you know that? Oh my god, outrageous! Do you even think?"

He heard Da-yong running away.

Feeling as if he had become like Sim the Blind Man in the old story, Myong-dok groped his way to the car door's handle and opened it. Once inside, he opened the glove compartment and took out some tissue paper and wiped the tears away. He sat and blinked for a long time. Then the blurry world began to return to its proper shape. He still waited for a long time, with the door open, without smoking, expecting Da-yong to come back. But she never did. She should have at least said good-bye as she left. What on earth has made her so intractable!

He closed the door and started the engine. Before driving out of the parking lot, he looked at the crescent moon through the car window. Since it was plumper than the day before, it must be waxing. It occurred to him that in the course of one day, from the previous one till now, he had seen the daytime moon in the morning, the afternoon, and the evening. He felt as if he had caught a glimpse of an entire life. He wondered: Why is it called the daytime moon, not the morning moon, afternoon moon, and evening moon? Then he answered to himself: any moon still visible after the sunrise is the daytime moon. The sun always meets the daytime moon. So, from the viewpoint of the sun, there is no moon at night. He drove out of the parking lot of the farmhouse.

창작노트
Writer's Note

사람이 사람을 만나는 최초의 순간에 대해 자주 생각한다. 한 사람에게서 관계라는 게 생성되는 태초의 시간. 그 시간의 지엄함, 그 최초의 각인에 대한 궁금증이 요즘 나를 사로잡고 있는 주제이다. 그것은 달리 말하면, 가족이다.

아버지와 딸은 묘한 관계이다. 어머니를 매개로 해서 맺어지는 관계이면서 어머니라는 장애를 극복해야 하는 관계이기도 하다. 어렵게 쓰고 싶지는 않다. 나는 딸이 아버지에 대해 느끼는 근원적인 거리감과 공포, 증오와 동경에 대해 알고 있다. 그러나 아버지가 되어보지 못했기 때문에, 앞으로도 영영 될 수 없기에 아버지가 딸에

I often think about the moment when one person for the first time meets another. The time when one's first ever relationship germinates, the solemnity of that time, what gets first inscribed in his or her memory—these are the subjects I ponder over these days. In this story, I am talking about a special kind of "first meeting" though: the relationship between members of a family.

While I had no intention of writing a complicated story, I found the relationship between a father and daughter to be quite intricate. For one thing, it is a relationship formed with the mother as at the same time a medium and an obstacle. I was also aware of the original feelings of aloofness, fear, hatred,

대해 느끼는 감정이 정확히 무엇인지는 알지 못한다. 내가 딸로서 겪어본 바에 의하면 아버지 역시 딸에게 묘한 거북함과 불편함, 경멸과 연민을 느끼는 듯하다.

우리 마음속에 애초에 생겨났던 것이 없어지는 건 불가능하다. 깨뜨린다고 해서 사라지지도 않는다. 파편과 잔해가 남을 뿐이다. 하지만 그럼에도 불구하고, 있던 것의 그 날카로운 모서리, 울퉁불퉁한 단면을 사포질하고 궁글리는 정도는 가능하지 않을까 싶다. 이 작품에서 나는 그런 작은 시도를 하는 아버지와 딸을 다루고자 했다. 물론 그들은 성공하지 못했으리라. 이 작품은 신화가 아니라 소설이니까. 그러나 그들이 실패한 것도 아니리라. 소설은 끝났지만 그들의 삶은 끝나지 않았으니까.

이 작품을 쓸 때 나는 토지문화관 105호에 있었다. 105호에서 나는 불면에 시달리며 딸을 기다리는 아버지를 썼고 막차가 들고 나는 소리를 들으며 캄캄한 밤 버스를 타고 읍내에 나가 아버지의 안주로 치즈와 과일을 사오는 딸을 썼다. 아롱이와 다롱이는 토지문화관이 있는 회촌 마을에서 만난 많은 개들로부터 왔다. 그 개들에게, 아울러 그 마을에 있던 모든 나무와 새들, 호수와 숲, 밭을 매던 이들에게 고맙고 정다운 마음을 전한다.

and yearning that a daughter can have toward her father. Since I will never be a father, I do not know exactly how a father feels toward a daughter; from my experience as a daughter, however, I can say this much: fathers also seem to feel toward their daughters a mixed sense of awkwardness, uncomfortableness, disdain, and compassion.

It is impossible for what has already come into being in our hearts to disappear. And breaking it up cannot make it vanish either, since it remains in the form of debris. Nevertheless, I believe the sharp and rough edges of strong emotions can be smoothed and made less jagged. In this story, I intended to depict a father and his daughter who try to make an attempt at minor changes in their relationship. Of course, they may not have succeeded in their attempt—it is because this is not a myth but a work of fiction. On the other hand, they may not have failed either—because even when a story comes to an end, the characters' lives are not over.

When I was writing this story, I was staying in Room 105 in Toji Cultural Center. Suffering from insomnia there, I created a father who waits for his daughter through the night, also suffering from insomnia; and hearing the last bus arriving and leaving, I portrayed a daughter who gets on a bus on a dark night to go into town to buy cheese and fruit for her father. As for Arong'ee and Darong'ee, I got inspiration from the many dogs that I met in Hoechon Village, where Toji Cultural Center is located. I would like to send warm greetings and thanks to those dogs, all the trees and birds, lakes and woods, and the people who worked in the fields of that village.

해설
Commentary

혼란과 무지 쪽으로의 퇴각

정홍수 (문학평론가)

권여선의 단편소설 「모르는 영역」을 읽고 나면 쉽게 의문이 떠오른다. 이 봄날의 1박 2일 동안 도대체 무슨 일이 일어난 건가. 소소하게 인물들의 마음을 건드리고 흔든 일이 없었던 것은 아니다. 무언가가 웅웅거리면서 소설의 시간 위로 부유한 것도 같다. 약간 성가시고 까칠한 상태로 말이다. 그러나 그것들은 또 정색하고 따져보거나 계속 품고 있기에는 어딘가 부족하거나 희미한 것들 같다. 혹은 약간의 나른함마저 풍기는 것들. 일상의 시간 저편으로 묽게 풀어져 사라져가는 것들. 그러니까 우리가 자주 그 존재를 잊는 '낮달' 같은 시간들.

그러나 무언가가 이 소설의 시간 위로 떠다니고 있다

Regression To Confusion and Ignorance

Jung Hongsoo (literary critic)

After reading "An Unknown Realm" by Kwon
Yeo-sun, one is likely to ask oneself a basic question: What on earth happened during those two
spring days? In fact, there *are* some trivial affairs
that goad or upset the characters in the story. One
is left with an impression that *some things*, having
been jarred loose and provoked, float up, droning,
beyond the novelistic time. At the same time, these
events are too vague and insufficient to scrutinize
or entertain with assurance. With even a hint of
languidness, they get diluted and slip away from
our everyday, temporal realm, into that of "the daytime moon," whose existence we often forget.

If we feel the need to look into the slightly goad-

고 하는 느낌, 그 약간의 성가심에 대해 생각해볼 필요를 느꼈다면, 그때 우리는 권여선이라는 특별한 소설의 기호 안으로 이미 한 발을 내디딘 셈이다. 그것은 또한 흐림과 갬 사이의 무수한 날씨, 대개는 의식하지 못한 채로 지나치는 인생의 미세한 '기압골/전선' 사이로 우리의 의식을 진입시키는 일이기도 하다.

"다영은 여주에 있다고 했다."(8쪽) 소설의 첫 문장이다. "여주라면 명덕이 공을 친 클럽에서 고속도로로 10분 남짓 걸리는 곳이었다."(8쪽) 행을 바꾸고 이어지는 두 번째 문장이다. 다영은 누구이고, 명덕은 누구인가. 이들은 무슨 관계인가. 알 수 없다. 다영 일행이 있는 여주의 한 식당에 명덕이 도착하기 전까지 우리에게 이들의 관계는 '모르는 영역'으로 남아 있다. 명덕이 신발도 벗지 않은 채 식당 출입문 안으로 머리를 들이밀자 다영의 말이 들려온다. "아빠 왔어?"(24쪽) 다영 일행인 산뜻한 젊은 여성의 목소리도 가세한다. "금방 고기 나온다니까 빨리 오세요, 아버님!"(24쪽) 이제 우리는 조금씩 알게 된다. 부녀는 지금 함께 살고 있지 않고, 둘 사이엔 이상한 서걱거림이 존재한다는 것을. 그렇다면 짧은 1박 2일의 시간 후에는 어떠한가? '모르는 영역'은 사라

ing things that hover above the temporal frame-work of this work of fiction, we have already taken a step into the world of novelistic semiotics specif-ic to Kwon Yeo-sun, the writer. Having done so, we also have let our consciousness open to the countless variations of weather between "cloudy" and "clear"—that is, to the subtle differences be-tween the "low-pressure troughs and weather fronts" in life that we remain unconscious of most of the time.

The story begins with the sentence "Da-yong said that she was in Yoju."(9) And the next sentence opens a new paragraph: "Yoju was about ten-min-ute freeway drive from the country club where Myong-dok had just played golf."(9) Who is Da-yong? Who is Myong-dok? What is the relationship between them? At first, we do not know. Their re-lationship is in the "unknown realm" until Myong-dok arrives at a restaurant in Yoju where Da-yong and her teammates are waiting for him. When Myong-dok, even before taking off his shoes, opens the entrance door and pokes his head into the hall, Da-yong says, "Hi, Dad, You're here."(27) Next comes a sonorous young woman's voice, "The meat will be served any minute now, so don't take too long, sir."(27) From here on, we are little

지는가? 독자의 자리에서도 그러하지만, 두 부녀 사이에도 '모르는 영역'은 여전히 남고, 오히려 좀더 미묘하고 복잡한 영역으로 넘어간 듯한 느낌을 준다.

소설은 아내의 죽음 후 더 소원해진 부녀의 관계를 짧은 봄날의 시간 안에서 보여주면서 '이해와 오해' 혹은 '근본적 무지(無知)'의 영역에 얽힌 인간사의 오랜 이야기 속으로 합류하는데, 여기서 문제는 그 영역 속으로 한발 한발 진입하는 권여선 소설의 예민한 촉수와 리듬, 문체의 미묘한 힘이 아닌가 한다. 명덕이란 인물이 겪고 있는 짜증과 혼란은 소설 초반부터 그 문체 수준에서 미묘한 물리적인 암시에 도달해 있다.

운동 후의 식사, 낮술의 취기, 봄날의 나른함이 겹쳐 그는 선잠에 빠지면서도 이게 어쩐지 저 은은한 낮달 때문이지 싶었고, 이게 죄다 저 뜯긴 솜 같은 낮달 때문입니다…… 낮달 때문입니다…… 하다 잠이 들었다.(10쪽)

그새 구름이 끼어 낮달은 보이지 않았고 허공에 꽃씨만 분분 날렸다. 테이블 위에 놓인 재떨이의 뚜껑이

by little let in on their relationship. The father and his daughter live separately; there is a sense of awkwardness between them. What then happens after the short period, one night and two days, that they spend together? Does the "unknown realm" become known? As a matter of fact, it remains on the part of the father and daughter—as well as for the reader. If anything, this realm seems to become subtler and more complicated.

By depicting a couple of short spring days, the story reveals the father's awkward relationship with his daughter, which has become aggravated after his wife's death. The story thus joins the long tradition of human dramas that originate from somewhere in-between understanding and misunderstanding, from the fundamentally unknowable. Here the writer's sensitiveness and narrative rhythm and style shine, enabling the story to take one step after another into the realm of those dramas. Already at the beginning, the writer's narrative style renders a subtle and physical implication of the father's fretfulness and confusion:

Because of the meal after golfing, the drink, and the lazy spring day, he felt drowsy and thought perhaps the lithe daytime moon was to

조금 열려 있어 그는 그 틈으로 꽃씨가 들어갈까봐 마음이 초조했다.(14쪽)

'뜯긴 솜 같은 낮달' '조금 열린 재떨이 뚜껑'은 작가가 인물의 감각과 언어로 도달한 세상의 처연하고 쓸쓸한 영역이고 봄날의 진정한 '사건'이다. 식당에서 빨간 신발 한 짝을 두고 벌어지는 소동은 '모르는 영역'을 둘러싸고 일어나는 인생의 흔한 소극(笑劇)을 압축하는데, 식당 주인이 흰 개를 추궁하고 야단치는 데서 인간의 무지와 편견에 정확히 조응한다. 더하여, 음식값을 놓고 식당 주인과 다영이 벌이는 실랑이 장면은 권여선 소설이 말과 상황의 세부에 얼마나 민감하고 철저한지 잘 예시해준다. "좋아요! 밥값은 낼 테니까 다섯 명분 팔만 원만 받으세요." "그게 무슨 소리야? 고기값이 얼마나 들었는데? 우리 아저씨가 고기만 오만 원어치를 끊어왔다고. 그러니까 이렇게 남아서들, 이렇게 싸가잖아 응?" "그럼 이거 안 싸가면 되잖아요?" "그건 아니지. 삶아논 거를, 그렇게는 안 되지."(38쪽)

이런 대목을 읽다보면 인생에서 이보다 더 절실하고 심각한 순간은 없는 것 같은데, 아니나 다를까 딸 다영

blame. It's all because of that torn-off, cotton ball of a moon, because of that daytime moon, he kept repeating, before he fell asleep.(11)

Only then did he realize that the sky had gotten cloudy and the daytime moon was no longer visible. Flower seeds were floating in the air. The lid of the ashtray on the table was ajar, which made him worry that the seeds might fall in it.(15-17)

Both "that torn-off, cotton ball of a moon" and "[t]he lid of the ashtray. . . ajar" belong to the sad and lonely realm of the world that the writer has reached by means of the character's senses and language. In fact, the torn-off moon and ashtray are the events that take place on that spring day. The scene in the restaurant of the "lost" red sneaker is a condensed version of the comedy that commonly occurs in life in connection with the "unknown realm," and the restaurant owner who scolds the white dog precisely corresponds with the ignorance and prejudice of a human. Moreover, the depiction of the quarrel between the restaurant owner and Da-yong about the bill demonstrates how sensitive and thorough Kwon is in her wording as well as depiction of the details of situations:

은 이 문제를 잊지 않고 있다가 명덕을 다시 추궁한다. "한 번이니까 괜찮다, 그냥 넘어가자…… 아버지는 그렇게 생각하시는 거네요? 그렇게 넘어가면 마음이 좋으세요? 한 번은, 한 번은…… 해도 됩니까?"(50쪽) 그러다 다시 한 번 묻는다. "왜 해도 됩니까, 한 번은?"(50쪽) 소설은 이 두 번째 반문 뒤의 상황을 이렇게 묘사한다. "다영은 느닷없이 깩 소리를 지르더니 흙 마당을 가로질러 뛰어갔다. 어디서 나타났는지 큰 개가 따라 뛰었고 덩달아 작은 개도 따라 뛰었다."(50쪽)

이 '한 번'은 그리고 다시 명덕에게 되돌아온다. 어둠이 깃드는 저수지 나뭇가지에 내려앉았다 돌연 가지를 박차고 날아간 새 한 마리의 사건으로.

멍하니 서서 새가 몰고 온 작은 파문과 고요의 회복을 지켜보던 그는 지금 무언가 자신의 내부에서 엄청난 것이 살짝 벌어졌다 다물렸다는 걸 깨달았다. (……) 그게 무엇인지 알 수 없지만 그에게 왔던 것은 이미 사라져버렸고 다시 반복되지 않을 것이고 영영 지울 수도 없으리라고 그는 침울하게 생각했다. 단 한 번이라니…… 단 한 번이었다니…… 다영도 이곳에서 이런

"Okay, we'll pay for the steamed rice, but the charge should be 80,000 won for the five of us."

"What're you talking about? Do you even know how much the pork cost us? My husband's bought 50,000 won's worth of it from the butcher. That's why you've this much leftover, right?"

"Then, we won't take these. Are you satisfied now?"

"No, that doesn't make sense. It's been already cooked. You can't do that."(41)

As readers, we can easily sense the heightened tension in this scene, as if nothing in life could be more serious. And, as expected, Da-yong doesn't forget it and later criticizes her father again:

"It's happened just once, so it's okay..."

"Just once, so it's no big deal, just forget about it—that's what you think? Do you really feel okay to smooth it over like that? If it's just once, people are allowed to do things like that—if they do it just once?"(53)

Da-yong then asks once more, "Why is it okay to do wrong, if it's just once?"(53) And she suddenly screams and runs away across the dirt yard. Out of

무섭도록 강렬한 한 번을 경험한 것일까.(54~56쪽)

　　그러니까 한 번은 해도 되는 게 아니라, 한 번이 다.
무섭도록 강렬한 한 번들. 그 무심한 집적이 인생이라는
걸 명덕도 다영도 권여선 소설도 알겠지만, 끝내 그 한
번은 '모르는 영역'으로 남으리라. 소설 「모르는 영역」은
그렇게 봄날에 찾아들었다 사라져가는, 다시는 반복되
지 않을 '한 번'의 시간을 채집하려는 불가능한 시도다.
소설 전체에 어떤 안간힘이 인물 모두에게, 밭에 비료를
뿌리는 반백의 두 남자와 텅 빈 들판에서 밭일을 하는
노파를 포함해 모두에게 공평하게 주어져 있지만, 소설
의 분위기가 조금씩 어긋나며 부조리한 슬픔으로 채워
지고 마는 것도 그래서이리라. 구린 퇴비 냄새와 다디단
꽃향기가 뒤섞인 봄날의 아침은 하룻밤 사이에 "와장창"
도착해 있지만 사람들은 여전히 서로 낯설고 어색한 채
서로를 모르는 가운데 또 하루를 시작해야 한다. 부녀간
에 도모된 약간의 이해와 다가섬은 더 많은 무지의 영
역을 남기고 닫으려 한다. 비문증을 앓고 있는 아버지
명덕에게 다시 떠오른 어제의 낮달은 잘 보이지 않는다.
"눈이 잘 안 보여요? 그럼 저기, 달 뜬 거 보여 안 보여?

nowhere, the dogs appear. The larger dog runs after her first, then the smaller dog follows.(53-55)

The word "once" boomerangs on Myong-dok later, when at nightfall he witnesses a bird alighting on a tree branch at the reservoir, only to abruptly launch off:

Standing there absently, witnessing the small stir brought about by the bird and the recovery of stillness, he realized that something stupendous had just opened and then closed again inside him. (...) He didn't know what had come over him, but he understood it was already gone, and would never be repeated or erased, and the thought made him feel gloomy. Only once in a lifetime—just this once and no more....When Da-yong came here, he wondered, did she also have this terribly intense, once-in-a-lifetime experience?(57-59)

It boils down to this: A mistake made just "once" is not to be tolerated because "once" is all there is. The truth is that life is a heedless accumulation of terrible, intense "onces." And all of them, that is, Myong-dok, Da-yong, and Kwon Yeo-sun's story

되게 예쁜 달인데." "달? 낮달이 또 떴어?" "안 보인다, 다 영아."(92쪽) 이 부녀간 문답은 참으로 슬프다.

이제 명덕은 "심봉사가 된 기분으로('심청전'의 '뺑덕어 멈'이 '명덕'의 이름 위로 겹친다. 이것은 소설이 할 수 있는 얼마 안 되는 슬픈 유희다) 더듬더듬" 차문을 열고 떠나려 한다. 명덕은 이 봄날의 여행이 시작되기 전보다 더 혼란스럽 고 더 무지한 쪽으로 밀려나 있다. 우리는 소설의 결말 에 동의할 수밖에 없다. 우리 역시 명덕처럼 소설을 읽 기 전보다 더 혼란스럽고 착잡한 자리로 옮겨가 있다. 그렇다면 이 짧은 봄날의 여행에서 승자는 누구인가. 권여선의 소설은 잠시 우리를 뒤흔들어놓고 사라져간 다. 저수지 나뭇가지에 착지했다 날아간 새가 몰고 온 작은 파문처럼. 권여선 소설은 정확히 이 파문이다. 우 리가 권여선 소설을 사랑하는 이유이기도 하겠다. 다음 은 소설의 마지막 문단이다.

그는 차문을 닫고 시동을 걸었다. 출발하려다 차창 너머로 초승달을 보았다. 어제보다 살이 더 오른 걸로 보아 바야흐로 차는 중인 것 같았다. 그러고 보니 어 제부터 오늘까지 그는 누군가의 인생을 일별하듯 아

itself, end up learning this truth once, but in the end *that* "once" remains always part of the unknown realm. The story "An Unknown Realm" is an impossible attempt to capture these "onces" that appear and vanish on one spring day, never to reappear. Perhaps that is why, despite the fact that the writer gives the same degree of utmost attention to all the characters, including two gray-haired men who fertilize the field and an old woman who works alone in the field, the general mood of the story becomes eroded, little by little, by discordance, until a sense of absurdity and sadness engulf the entire story. The spring morning, filled with both the stink of compost and sweet fragrance of flowers, arrives overnight with a great "crash"; but the main characters start another day feeling unacquainted and awkward with one another. Although the father and daughter attempt to understand and come closer to each other, in the end they are about to close their hearts again, leaving a larger unknown realm between them. Suffering from the floaters in his eyes, Myong-dok cannot see the daytime moon that he was able to in the previous day.

"You can't see well? Can you see the daytime moon up there? It's very beautiful."

침, 오후, 저녁의 낮달을 모두 보았다. 왜 아침달 낮달 저녁달이 아니고 모두 낮달인가 생각하다, 해 뜨고 뜬 달은 죄다 낮달인 게지, 생각했다. 해는 늘 낮달만 만나고, 그러니 해 입장에서 밤에 뜨는 달은 영영 모르는 거지, 그런 생각을 하며 그는 농가 펜션의 주차장을 빠져나왔다.(94~96쪽)

정말 '영영' 모르고 마는 걸까.

정홍수 문학평론가. 평론집 『소설의 고독』 『흔들리는 사이 언뜻 보이는 푸른빛』, 산문집 『마음을 건다』가 있다.

"Moon...a daytime moon is out again?"

"I can't see, Da-yong."(98-99)

This dialog between father and daughter saddens us greatly. Now Myong-dok, "feeling as if he had become like Sim the Blind Man in the old story, groped his way" to open the car door. (One of the characters in "The Story of Sim Chong" is called Bbaeng-dok's mother. Myong-dok and Bbaeng-dok have "dok" in common. This is one of the games that fiction can play.) Myong-dok feels more confused and unknowing than before his setting out on this journey on one spring day. We cannot help agreeing to the story's ending of unknowingness. After reading this story, we also feel confused and perturbed. Who then is the beneficiary in this brief spring-day journey and encounter? Kwon's story disturbs our minds for a while and then disappears. Like the repercussions caused by the little bird's alighting on and departing from a tree branch near the reservoir, her fiction is a repercussion. This is the reason why we love Kwon's works of fiction. The story "An Unknown Realm" ends:

He closed the door and started the engine. Before driving out of the parking lot, he looked at the crescent moon through the car window.

Since it was plumper than the day before, it must be waxing. It occurred to him that in the course of one day, from the previous one till now, he had seen the daytime moon in the morning, the afternoon, and the evening. He felt as if he had caught a glimpse of an entire life. He wondered: Why is it called the daytime moon, not the morning moon, afternoon moon, and evening moon? Then he answered to himself: any moon still visible after the sunrise is the daytime moon. The sun always meets the daytime moon. So, from the viewpoint of the sun, there is no moon at night. He drove out of the parking lot of the farmhouse.(100)

Will the nocturnal moon remain unknown to the sun forever?

Jung Hongsoo Jung Hongsoo is a South Korean literary critic. His published books include two collections of critical essays, *Solitude of Fiction* and *Blue Seen Briefly While Swaying*, and a collection of essays, *Betting My Mind*.

비평의 목소리
Critical Acclaim

'허구'가 만들어낸 베일을 걷어내고 들여다보면, 권여선의 소설 속 인물들은 하나같이 약하고, 겁 많고, 자기 앞가림도 못한 채 흔들리는 보통 사람들일 뿐이다. 그들은 술에 취했거나, 어리숙하게 속아 인생을 망치거나, 난데없는 불운을 만나 스러질 운명을 지닌, 곧 이름마저 잊히는 우리 자신의 모습이다. 작가는 왜 이들을 돌아보고, 응시하고, 파편처럼 흩어진 기억들을 모아서 이야기로 만드는가. 누군가 우리에게 맡겨버린, 왜 짊어지고 가야 하고 느닷없이 내려놓아야 하는지 도무지 알 수 없는 인생살이에 의미를 부여하기 위해서가 아니겠는가. 나는 이것이야말로 바로 권여선의 소설이 세상과 사람들을 구원

Behind the fictional facade, the characters in Kwon Yeo-sun's stories are all weak, timid, confused ordinary people who are unable to take care of themselves. They are usually either drunk, or likely to be deceived by others, and thereby ruin their lives, or destined to encounter some unforeseen misfortunes and end up having not only themselves but their names disappear and forgotten; in other words, they are the very images of us. Why then does the writer pay attention to them, gaze at them, and weave the scattered debris of their memories into narrative? Isn't it to give a meaning to our life that someone has imposed on us and that we have to carry on our back until we

하는 방식이라고 생각한다. 권여선의 소설에서 가장 감동적인 장면은, 이야깃감도 못 될, 비루하기 짝이 없는 우리네 인생들이 아름답게 되살아나는 모습이다.

이소연, 「인생은 아름답다, 권여선식으로─권여선의 최근 단편에 대한 소고」,
《작가세계》, 작가세계, 2016.

권여선은 누구보다도 내면의 서사를 구축하는 데 탁월한 능력과 성취를 보여준 작가이다. 그녀의 소설이 겨냥하는 초점은 구체적인 사건의 발생이나 전개가 아니라 사소해 보이기까지 한 일상의 작은 파편으로부터 비롯된 정동의 강도와 흐름에 맞춰져 있다. 내면을 채우는 여러 정념과 욕망, 그리고 내면으로부터 발아하는 관계의 만화경에 대한 묘사야말로 권여선 소설을 읽게 만드는 근원적 힘이 되는 경우가 많다. 생동감 넘치는 문장으로 형상화한 인간들처럼 기괴하면서도 동시에 일상의 실감에 부합하는 인물은 우리 소설사에서 발견하기 힘든 것이었다.

이경재, 「기억의 윤리」, 《작가세계》, 작가세계, 2016.

are suddenly forced to put down for some incomprehensible reasons? I believe this is the way chosen by Kwon to redeem through her works the world and the people in it. The most moving scenes in her stories are those where our trivial and miserable lives get beautifully revived.

Lee So-yeon, "Life Is Beautiful, in Kwon Yeo-sun's Own Way: An Inquiry into Kwon Yeo-sun's Recent Short Stories," *Writers' World* (Seoul: Writers' World, 2016)

Kwon Yeo-sun is remarkable for her unsurpassable ability to construct the internal narrative. Her novels focus not on the beginning and development of concrete events but on the intensity and flow of emotions that are triggered by small, even trivial-looking fragments of everyday life. What fundamentally draws us into the world of Kwon's fiction is often the depiction of various passions and desires that occupy the inner self, and the kaleidoscope of relations germinating from *that* inner self. The strange, yet realistic, ordinary characters embodied by Kwon's animated narrative have been rare in our history of the novel.

Lee Kyung-jae, "The Ethics of Memory," *Writers' World* (Seoul: Writers' World, 2016)

K-픽션 020
모르는 영역

2018년 1월 8일 초판 1쇄 발행

지은이 권여선 | 옮긴이 전미세리 | 펴낸이 김재범
기획위원 전성태, 정은경, 이경재
편집 김형욱, 신아름 | 관리 강초민, 홍희표 | 디자인 나루기획
인쇄·제책 AP프린팅 | 종이 한솔PNS
펴낸곳 (주)아시아 | 출판등록 2006년 1월 27일 제406-2006-000004호
주소 경기도 파주시 회동길 445(서울 사무소: 서울특별시 동작구 서달로 161-1 3층)
전화 02.821.5055 | 팩스 02.821.5057 | 홈페이지 www.bookasia.org
ISBN 979-11-5662-173-7(set) | 979-11-5662-337-3(04810)
값은 뒤표지에 있습니다.

K-Fiction 020
An Unknown Realm

Written by Kwon Yeo-sun | Translated by Jeon Miseli
Published by ASIA Publishers | 445, Hoedong-gil, Paju-si, Gyeonggi-do, Korea
(Seoul Office:161-1, Seodal-ro, Dongjak-gu, Seoul, Korea)
Homepage Address www.bookasia.org | Tel.(822).821.5055 | Fax.(822).821.5057
First published in Korea by ASIA Publishers 2017
ISBN 979-11-5662-173-7(set) | 979-11-5662-337-3(04810)

금기와 욕망 Taboo and Desire

바이링궐 에디션 한국 대표 소설 set 6

운명 Fate

미의 사제들 Aesthetic Priests

식민지의 벌거벗은 자들 The Naked in the Colony

바이링궐 에디션 한국 대표 소설 set 7

백치가 된 식민지 지식인 Colonial Intellectuals Turned "Idiots"